Knave of Hearts

Knave of Hearts

Stories

Mark Smith

BLUE WEST BOOKS

RIVERSIDE, CALIFORNIA

Blue West Books
Riverside, California

Copyright © 2013, Mark Smith

Printed in the United States of America
First edition, 2013

Several stories in this collection were previously published in these or earlier versions in the following publications: *Elements, Epiphany, Intertext, Lone Star Literary Quarterly, Pacific Coast Journal, Pinehurst Journal,* and *Sulpher River Literary Quarterly.*

ISBN: 978-0-9859495-0-1
LCCN: 2012919533

Blue West Books is a publishing collective dedicated to promoting emerging and established authors of contemporary fiction, poetry, and essays in California and the Southwest.

www.BlueWestBooks.com

For Catharine and Peter, the stars in my night.

Contents

Knave of Hearts

Marty

Pacing around this hospital waiting room, I'm thinking, where does any story start? Can you say where yours started? In the first place, none of us can remember being born or even the first few years of life. Earliest thing most of us can remember is about age three, three-and-a-half. Think how long three years is. Three whole years out of your life—years when you learn to eat, sleep, walk and talk—none of us can remember any of that.

Starting to get my point? Now I'll tell you that I know lots of people who couldn't tell you what happened to them last week. I mean, these people all walking around eating and talking and working and they can't remember what they ate for dinner last night, what they said to you last time they saw you, or what it is they are supposed to be working for. Sleepwalkers, that's what they are.

But guess what. They never shake off that snooze. They get married, have kids, buy a house, make a fortune some of them, and when they're done doing all that, they put their affairs in order and check out. But what's the point? They've been dead all along.

Such a guy is my partner Marty Grace. Marty and I read water meters. We're a team. We spend eight hours a day together; have for five years now. I had another partner before Marty. His name was Stitch. Stitch was a nice guy, quiet, a family man. Kept his nose clean. Never would go for a beer after work. Liked to save his money and keep healthy. He was always worried as hell that he'd get old and sick and use up his insurance and not be able to pay his bills. Then one night while he was watching TV, he fell over dead without saying a word. Next time I saw his wife, she was driving a brand new Oldsmobile.

So after Stitch died, I got Marty. Now don't get me wrong, Marty's a nice guy. I love him like my brother. Would I be wearing out the carpet in this goddam hospital at three in the morning if I didn't? But I read a lot, always did. Used to have big hopes for myself, like maybe I might go to college one day and make something of myself. And when I used to plan out my life, I never thought I'd end up spending forty hours a week with a guy the likes of Marty. But, Christ, it could be worse. I could have AIDS, or be homeless, or live in Haiti or some damn place. Could definitely be worse.

So I go out reading meters with Marty. We read meters for the Passaic Water Company. We work the town of Bergenhurst, New Jersey. I always marvel at how they got it worked out. Town of about 20,000 people, just under 11,000 meters. It takes us exactly twenty working days to read all those meters so that every twenty-eight days, we start back at scratch. I think that's pretty amazing, but Marty never caught on.

We started out this morning just like every morning, with coffee at the deli. Marty piled up his usual breakfast: egg and bacon on a roll with ketchup, a package of cinnamon donuts, a container of chocolate milk, and a coffee regular extra sweet. Carmine who runs the deli always tells him, "Jeez, Marty, you pregnant or what? Looks like you're eatin' for two." He says this nearly every morning and every time he says it, the guys at the counter crack up like they never heard it before; Marty too.

Me, I ordered coffee black and a butter roll. We got back in the truck and Marty starts feeding his face. He says, "What streets we doin' today?"

I say, "The same damn streets we did twenty-eight days ago."

He looks at me blank, and I say, "Ain't you got it figgered out yet?"

"Got what figgered out?"

"The route, Einstein, the route. How long you been on this job?"

"Five years this March," says Marty, his cheeks bulged with egg and roll.

"Five years and you ain't figgered out yet that they give us the same streets—the same meters—every twenty-eighth friggin' day?"

Marty dips a donut in his coffee and then in his mouth and says, "I guess I never noticed. What difference does it make anyway?"

"The difference it makes, genius, is that guys like Dayton and Del'Italia got our lives worked out to a precise science. They know where we are every damn minute of the day."

"Dayton, he's the one I hate, that damned moulie bastard," Marty says, missing the point of everything I just said.

"And that's why they get to sit in an office all day while meatheads like us gotta walk our asses off for a third of the pay." I finish my coffee, jam the waxed paper from around the roll in the cup, put the lid back on and squeeze the whole thing into a little ball. "So today it's Stuyvesant over to the river and then all the way down to the Kings supermarket and we're late so finish your breakfast and let's get started."

But Marty forgot to buy his lottery ticket so he took a minute and ran back into the deli. Every day Marty buys a lottery ticket and every damn day I bust his stones about it. He got back to the truck and threw it on the seat.

"Why the hell do you do that," I say.

"Do what?" he says.

"Buy them damn tickets. That's just a sucker's game. Another way for the rich to get our money selling us a worthless slip of paper."

"Aw hell, it's only a dollar," Marty says.

"A dollar," I say. "What number did you pick?"

"My birthday, same as always," says Marty.

"That seems appropriate," I say.

So we split up our streets and, as usual, I got done with mine a little sooner than Marty and I stood waiting for him at noon at the corner of Stuyvesant and Post, a block from the Kings. I leaned against a red Chrysler with a white convertible top parked at the curb and thought, where the hell do they get the money to buy these cars?

Then I saw Marty coming down the block. I watched him as he trudged along in his uniform, taking his own sweet time and thought, hurry the fuck up, Marty. Finally, he got to the last house across the street from where I was standing and he flashed me the high sign and went over to the meter in the yard of the house.

He looked at the meter and wrote down the number and started to walk toward the street. Then he waved his hand around his face like he was slapping off a bug. He was within earshot now standing in the driveway and he said, "Damn bees're ever'where." I started to stroll over to where he was standing and he slapped his neck. He said, "Jeez, I think I got stung." Then, before I could say anything, this look came over his face and he made this little funny choking sound down in his throat. He bent over to put his hands on his knees like he was going to throw up. Before I knew it, he had dropped onto the driveway.

I knew right away what was wrong: he's allergic to bees.

I pulled out my cell and called 911. They got there really fast and took us both to the hospital where I been waiting ever since. A nurse came out a little before six and told me that Marty was in intensive care and asked if his family had been informed. I said Marty was single just like me. She just nodded and said I should go home for a while since there was nothing to do.

I should have gone home. That way I never would've been standing around in the waiting room watching the television when they had the lottery drawing. When that pretty lady started to turn those little Ping-Pong balls with the numbers around and read them off, I thought I was hearing things. Then there it was, flashed up on the screen in big white numbers underneath the Ping-Pong balls: Marty's birthday.

I went out to the parking lot of the hospital and got the ticket off the seat of my truck where Marty left it. I read it just to be sure.

I crumpled it up and started to fling it into the parking lot. Then I unwadded it and carefully smoothed out all the wrinkles. I put it in my pocket and came back inside the hospital to wait for Marty.

Sometimes it seems like I'm always waiting for Marty.

Snapper

As if it weren't weird enough to be trying to put a snapping turtle the size of a manhole cover into a flimsy plastic dry-cleaning bag, the plan after that seemed to involve transferring the beast to a shopping cart they had dragged from the supermarket several blocks away.

My wife and son and I were going for one of our tedious afternoon trips to the local swimming pool. Not exactly my idea of fun, I might quickly add, being dragged into the cold water every day to get shivering wet with a bunch of screaming kids peeing in the pool. Then, to witness the bizarre and cruel spectacle of these kids dicking around with this turtle, and the thing getting obviously more pissed off every minute. I stood there watching, dumbstruck, thinking that it would serve these kids right to have this monster bite off one of their fingers or whatever. My wife and son stepped up beside me.

"Hey!" said my wife. "What are those kids doing?" Though she could see what they were doing as well as I could.

"I think they're trying to put a snapping turtle into a dry-cleaning bag," I said. "Of course, I could be wrong."

"Wow, Dad," said my kid. "That's a big turtle." Which isn't as dumb a comment as it sounds since he's only four. And it *was* a big turtle. Biggest fucking turtle I ever saw. At least a foot across its gnarled shell and weighing, I would guess, twenty, twenty-five pounds. A noble beast, actually, something like a natural treasure. Not that I'd know a natural treasure if it bit me on the dick. Still, I appreciated that turtle. I felt sorry for it being dragged out of its element by this bunch of cretinous kids.

I felt like I ought to do something to stop them from terrorizing the thing though by all rights it ought to have been them who were scared. I'm absolutely sure that I would never have gone screwing around with an animal that big and mean when I was their age, which I judged to be around seven or eight. On the other hand, these kids were a bad element. I'd seen them abandoned to their own devices in the park on more than one occasion. Residents, no doubt, of the trailer park down on Congress Avenue by the park at Live Oak where the homeless hang out passing quarts of Colt 45. Hell, for all I knew, those homeless *were* their parents.

So I finally decided that I had some kind of moral obligation to stop these kids from killing this turtle.

"Hey, kids," I yelled. "Don't do that."

The oldest boy, a lanky, dirty urchin dressed only in dingy swimming trunks, glowered up at me from his crouched position.

The other kids turned cold, stupid eyes on me. Obviously they weren't used to having adults tell them what to do.

"Why not?" said the boy.

"That thing'll bite your finger off." Now I didn't really care about those kids or their smudgy fingers and anyway, I could tell that this sluggish old reptile was in little danger of biting anyone. In the first place, they were handling the thing by the tail and shell, which I seem to remember hearing is the way you are supposed to handle snapping turtles if you have to handle them at all. In the second place, the kids seemed to be sure enough of themselves that they couldn't get hurt, though that could have just been street smarts. After all, they were trying to put the thing in a dry-cleaning bag and a grocery cart. What kind of outdoorsmanship is that, for Christ's sake?

"Aw, we ain't been bit yet," sneered the boy. I guess this made some kind of logical sense to him.

"That's why we're holding it by the tail," said another child, a girl I'd often seen hanging around the pool trying to chum up to the life guards.

"What're you going to do with it?" asked my wife.

"Take it home," shrugged one of the kids. Stupid question. Of course, every home ought to have at least one viscious reptile lurking around under the furniture or sleeping under the car.

"Keep it for a pet," said the girl.

"Daddy," my son piped up. "Can we get a turtle like that for a pet?"

I laughed and touseled his hair. Right, I thought, my kid, who's deathly afraid of the neighbors' Jack Russell terrier that's about as ferocious as the Pillsbury doughboy, is going to take a snapping turtle, of all damned things, home and feed it—what? Purina Turtle Chow?

"Where are your parents, anyway?" I asked. A question that had been on my mind for weeks. Just then, as if on cue, a woman's voice boomed up behind us: "What the hell are you doing with that thang?" I turned to see the mother stepping carefully across the pebbled parking lot on her bare feet. She was hugely obese and wore a flowered bathing suit. She looked identical to the girl, who seemed only a scale model of her mother—like those dolls from the Ukraine that fit one inside the other.

"Takin' it home," snarled the boy, shooting daggers at this woman who must have been his mother, too, since he also looked like her. *Probably his mother and his aunt, too,* I thought. *That way he gets those genes from both sides.*

"You let go of that thang rat this minute, you hear me, boy!"

"I ain't!" yelled the boy, still holding the turtle's jagged tail. The other children—only two that I could count, though I could have sworn there had been more—nervously shifted their eyes from the woman to the boy. They seemed to be trying to figure out which one of the two was the least likely to get crazy enough to hurt someone.

The turtle seemed oblivious to the whole controversy. It sat on the ground as solid as a fire hydrant, a mass of twigs, dry leaves and dirt lodged behind its claws from being dragged along the ground up from the creek. Occasionally, it would snap its beaked mouth suddenly and erratically from side to side or over its huge back shell. I understood completely. Why fucking bother? Easier to get dragged along by the tail by someone else than to put up a fight.

What good did it get you anyway? Bide your time and look for your chance to make a getaway.

So I stood there at the edge of the parking lot, siding with the turtle against all odds, until my wife pulled on the towel draped over my shoulder and said, "Come on, let's go."

I glanced at the turtle once more. I felt like I ought to make some kind of stand. Go down into the creek bed and stage a heroic rescue. Intimidate the kids and their mother until they fled. But who would really do that, except for an animal rights activist or something? And I'll bet even the most hardcore Earth Firsters might back off if they got a load of this charming family.

"Fuck it," I muttered under my breath and fell in step behind my wife.

As we walked away, mama yelled, "You put that dayum thang back in the crick or I ain't never buyin' you another goddamn toy ever. You hear me?" Jesus, I thought, remembering all those touchy-feely classes in parenting techniques my wife had ever dragged me to. But I chuckled to myself, certain that her crude logic (was it a bribe or a threat?) would work its magic on these kids and they would give up the fight and let this old creature lumber back into the murky waters of Stacy Creek where it belonged. The other children started back toward the pool, bored with this business.

A few minutes later, beside the pool, the fat girl was telling the lifeguard about the turtle. The lifeguard looked bored. Later, with my family happily bobbing in the water, swim ring, beach ball and all, I gave into an urge to brave the fire ants on the grassy slope beside the pool and peer through the chain link fence to check on the turtle.

I got to the fence just in time to see the boy, alone now, single-minded in his resolve, hoist the turtle into the shopping cart. Then, like Sisyphus pushing his rock, he leaned into the handle of the cart and off they went, jingling slowly across the rutted parking lot and out onto the blacktop leading uphill toward their mutual fate.

Meals on Wheels

From inside Ruby's air-conditioned car, I stare out at a marquee on a pole in the parking lot of the Long Horn Meat Co. The sign reads,

HOT GUT
159

I wonder darkly at the sign's occult meanings: what is hot gut? 159? How hot? Gut of what? Is it even edible and under what conditions? I imagine it eaten in the busted linoleum kitchens of dim, undershirt-smelling houses where men cluster around a Formica table crowded with beer bottles and bowls of chopped tomatoes and onions.

Ruby drives on, noticing nothing, of course. I think she'd comment on it if she ever did, but we've driven by the sign once a week for nearly two years and she's never mentioned it. Ruby is my co-worker. We share adjacent cubicles in a sterile, fluorescent-lighted office where we work at jobs that are different but the same in ways, one of which being that they are essentially unimportant (this, I admit, is probably my view only). So we have developed, Ruby and I, a sort of home-away-from-home camaraderie that stands us in good stead on Mondays when we do our route for Meals on Wheels.

Ruby fails to notice the "hot gut" sign this week because she is busy describing her latest obsession—total body workout. "I've decided that I'll focus on three strategic areas: my flabby upper arms, my flabby abdomen and my flabby butt." She laughs.

"Oh, please," I say. "You don't need to worry about that. You only weigh a hundred pounds."

"I'm up to fifteen minutes a day on the Nordic Track. I figure if I can get up to twenty minutes, I'll achieve my optimum goal in eight weeks instead of the usual ten."

"It's important to have goals for personal growth and development," I say.

"Are you making fun of me?"

"Me?"

"Yeah, you, buster. But I forgot; you're too busy with your intellectual pursuits to have any time for something as mundane as exercise."

"I'm busy all right, but nothing more intellectual than Sesame Street."

"Oh, right. Mr. Family Man."

"You got it."

We pull into the lot of the Meals on Wheels central kitchen. It's 11:35 a.m. The lunch rush is just starting. Women and men in office clothes are pouring out of their late model cars, ready to fill up their styrofoam coolers with meals bound for the mostly black mostly elderly "clients." It's 100 degrees out on this sunny parking lot, but everyone is happy. Our chins are held high at the thought of spending half an hour a week volunteering because no one else we know spends a full hour.

Inside we give Sally our route number and she announces to her assistant, "Six regular, two blue and a skim." In the shake of a lamb's tail we're backing out the door with our own coolers, one filled with square tin pie plates with paper tops while in the other are our cold bags (milk, juice, and an individually plastic-wrapped slice of white bread). The smell of institutional food permeates Ruby's car.

"Ah, smells good today," she says.

"It's awful. It's really a shame that old folks have to eat this swill in the autumn of their years."

"Don't think about it. Let's go."

And we're off on the route.

Ruby's not ready to drop the topic of her exercise program. "You just don't understand about growing old."

"Ah, sheesh. Don't give me this growing old crap again. I never knew anyone who worried about that as much as you do."

"And why shouldn't I? I'm old as blazes. A girl needs to take care to keep up her appearance."

"Oh. Yeah, I forgot. But then I'm married. That's the best thing about being married—you can let yourself go."

"That's gross," says Ruby. "I'm going to tell Emily you said that."

We drive past an abandoned building on an overgrown lot with a hand-painted sign that says, THE RAMBO HOTEL. The windows are boarded up with big squares of plywood and the wood siding has weathered to a uniform silver-gray.

"Next time we have customers in town let's put them up at the Rambo Hotel," says Ruby. I laugh. Of course, this is our standard, weekly joke. It's funny, Ruby never fails to notice *that* sign.

We turn onto a weedy, declining, unused street with the ill-fitting name of New York Avenue and find Mr. Jackson's house, a tiny bungalow with a shaded carport under which there is always a well-tended two-tone gold and white Impala of mid-80s vintage. Incongruously, there is a gas light standing in the front yard, a relic from the days when it was all the rage to put a gas light in your front yard, back when Mr. Jackson would've been 25 years younger and able to get his own meals.

Going up the front steps, with the hot plate and blue bag (soft mechanical), I notice his house has been treated to a new coat of paint, white, with the trim painted a nice chocolate brown. On cue, as usual, the instant I hit the steps, Mr. J. is there, pushing open the screen door. He's waiting, of course, probably since 10:30, though whether from hunger or politeness, I can't tell. He greets me in his permanently bent-over, Japanese-style bow and nearly inaudible voice that is more a loud sigh than actual words: "Uhhhnnn."

I leave the meal on a little table inside the door. In the dark room, I am aware of the shapes of the furniture: sofa, La-Z-Boy, television, the whole scene every bit as lonesome as a lost hound with not one speck of clutter to suggest any time at all is spent in this room, no doubt the biggest of the house.

Having deposited the meal, I back out in my own Asian bow. On an impulse, I say, "Got your home painted I see."

Mr. Jackson seems to smile, but I can't be sure. "Uhhnn-hunng," he says.

"Looks good," I say.

"Unnhhh," he says, retreating inside. This is more of a conversation than I've ever had with him and I stroll back to the car whistling.

"His house looks nice," says Ruby, inside her refrigerated car. This she would notice—any change in the status in the lives of the folks on our route. She's fond of Mr. Jackson. We both are. Once when he was off the list for two weeks she inquired and found that he had been in the hospital for several days. Dutifully, we went to see him but were turned away by a suspicious floor nurse wondering, no doubt, what business two youngish white folks in office clothes had with the likes of Mr. J.

The next delivery is next door so Ruby leaves the engine idling, tapping her palms on the wheel to the tune of some cowpunk sing-along on the radio, while I fetch another tin plate and blue cold bag.

I cross the sun-scorched weed patch of Mrs. Elma Snyder's house and knock at one of two identical screen doors. I wait, watching the street. Two houses away, a man of about sixty in a pork pie hat and khaki pants and shirt steps onto his front porch and looks down the street at me. I raise my hand. He returns the wave, then skedaddles back in to his air-conditioning.

No one answers my knock, though I hear voices inside. I knock again, this time on the other door. the voices lower and I hear steps approaching. The burglar-barred inner door jerks open and a huge woman in a bright orange and purple silk dress appears in the door. She looks about fifty, large with enormous breasts held in place by some industrial contraption the underwires of which make her boobs look like two huge dirigibles. She is wearing lots of big gold jewelry and she's smiling like she just scored big in the pick-6.

This is not Mrs. Snyder by any stretch. We M.O.W. volunteers are instructed to ask to see the client. I decline, not because I think I would discover Elma Snyder's hapless body stashed under the bed while her lazy offspring scarf down pie-panfulls of pre-masticated chicken, but that her daughter might think I think that.

"I'm so sorry to keep you waiting," she says, pushing the door open. Her fingernails are painted pink champagne. "We was just havin' church." Her eyes have disappeared into little slits of abundant amusement. She scoops the food from my hands and in a heartbeat she's gone and I'm back in the front seat of Ruby's Subaru wagon.

We head up New York, then turn onto Mount Calm Street. Next stop: Florence Cantor.

"So how's it going with that guy, that Chuck?"

"I don't know anyone named Chuck and I would probably shoot myself if I did."

"Don't be a smart ankle. You know who I mean."

"Yeah. You mean Jeff and you never get his name right. He's a nice guy. He makes me laugh."

"You can't ask for more than that" (I'm pretty sure I don't believe this). "What does he do for a living?"

"He's a repo man."

"You're kidding."

"No. He works for a bank repossessing cars, boats, whatever."

"What?"

"Yeah. He carries a gun to work. Can you believe that?"

Ruby pulls up at the curb of a white wood frame house with neat black shutters, cast iron railing, and a shady front porch lushly crowded with potted plants. All in all the place is as shipshape as a Quaker church.

Ruby takes Mrs. Cantor her meal. This always entails a long wait on the porch while Mrs. Cantor makes her long painful trip from the back of the house to the front, then a further wait as she unclicks three deadbolts. Ruby stands on the porch, sunglasses in one hand and the meal in the other. She's wearing a full linen skirt with pink flowers and a pink sash belt, as summery as lemonade.

I think about her repo man boyfriend depositing his hog leg, holster and all, on her bedside table of an evening. For some reason the thought makes me queasy. Mrs. Cantor appears in her screen door. I can see her stoop down to unfasten a knee-high eye hook, then one further up. I can imagine the conversation. Ruby says, "how are you," and Mrs. Cantor says, "Oh, honey. I ain't feelin' too well today. I'm real stiff." She might even ask after Ruby's husband—meaning me. She thinks we're married and even though we've both told her, at different times, that we're not—at least to each other—she has persisted in this notion that seems harmless enough since she doesn't even know our names.

In fact, none of our clients, past or present, have ever once asked our names or shown any curiosity about who we are. And why should they? Their lives are full enough with their dubious prospects for survival to waste one angstrom of mental effort on us. It's an arrangement I'm perfectly happy with and, if I had to guess, so is Ruby.

But Ruby lingers on Mrs. Cantor's porch, chatting. I bet I know what about: a small painted and glazed piggy pot borrowed empty two weeks ago and returned last week filled with an orange-topped Christmas cactus, just the kind of random act of kindness those obnoxious bumper stickers urge us to practice. Mrs. Cantor was suitably appreciative.

Ruby bounds back to the car, frisky as a kitten. "She says to thank my husband for the plant, too." She starts the car and pulls away from the curb.

"Did you?" I ask, grinning.

"I will if I ever have one which I hope is never."

"Now I'm confused. Do you want a man in your life or not?"

"*You're* confused." Ruby says. "Speaking of marriage, I've been meaning to ask you how it is that Emily puts up with you. You're so moody."

"I'm moody? That's funny, I always thought of myself as kind of happy-go-lucky."

"Well, not lately. You're always bitching about something or other: your job, the heat, your kid, your kid's teacher, whatever. You worry too much."

She turns on Milam and drives two blocks then turns left on 4th, destination Mr. Tibbs.

"Come to think of it, you're right," I say. "It sucks to be me."

We roll to a stop in front of Mr. Tibbs's house where, true to every expectation, Mr. Tibbs is sitting on a lawn chair in the scant shade of his front porch. He is a thin man, mid-60s, wearing bib overalls, limp cotton work shirt, and ancient Red Wing boots.

Today, however, there is a change: two kids, a boy and girl no older than 10, are playing on the dead-grass front yard. As I climb out of the car, they grow suddenly serious and move aside, where they stand, hands at their sides, watching me warily.

"Hey, kids!" I say in my breeziest voice. They stare at me in silence. "Hi, there, Mr. Tibbs."

"H'lo," says Mr. Tibbs, nodding. He's a man of few words, though all of them seem to be courtly polite. He turns his hands palm up, though they continue to rest on his thighs.

"You okay today?" I ask, laying his meal in his hands.

"Just fine, thank you," he says. "And yourself?"

"Fine, fine," I say, turning back toward the car.

"Y'all have a nice day," says Mr. Tibbs.

"You, too," I call over my shoulder. "Bye, kids!" I say to the boy and girl who stand side-by-side like soldiers. I think they haven't taken their eyes off me since I arrived.

After my door is shut, Ruby says, "They call him Mistah Tibbs," in her best Sidney Poitier voice, which might be mistaken for James Earl Jones or Billy Dee Williams. This is another regularly scheduled gag I had thought I would avoid this week. I laugh, but I must not sound very enthusiastic since Ruby says, "they seem like nice kids."

"Yeah. It must be nice to have calm and obedient children."

"Now don't start with that. Josh is a good kid, he's just a little high-strung."

"That's no surprise. Both his parents are high-strung."

"You're all highstrung, is what you're saying."

"Yeah. It's a high-strung house."

"Well, you can't pick your family," says Ruby.

"That's for damn sure. But I have a great family. I'm very lucky."

"Right," says Ruby with a far-away lilt to her voice. Suddenly, Ruby is bored with this conversation and has become as abstracted as a cloud. This occurs from time to time and there's no other solution but to reel her back in with something absolutely temporal.

"Did you ever read that book I—?"

"No," she interrupts, "I doubt it."

"How do you know what I was going to ask?"

"I've never read any of those books you've read. And unless it's set in the Southwest, I probably won't."

"You're kidding."

"No."

"You only read books about the Southwest?"

"*Set* in the Southwest."

"But why?" I wasn't aware of this and, in fact, tend to disbelieve it outright. Though it is true that over the years, I have recommended to Ruby dozens of books almost none of which has she ever read.

"Oh, well, nothing else really interests me."

I don't know whether to believe her or not. Finally I choose to drop it and pretend it's one of Ruby's perverse jokes designed, ultimately, to make fun of me. The alternative is too disturbing.

While I'm busy brooding about Ruby's reading habits, we drive by Donny's, a storefront walk-in grocery with burglar bars on the windows and a pay phone on the wall outside that is always in use. This corner is the only part of our route that seems menacing in the gangsta hard way that folks who never visit this part of town think about it. Once upon a more innocent time, the store might have been a safe and respectable midday destination for a stay-at-home mom to push a stroller, or the kind of place a husband on his way home might stop for a loaf of bread and a quart of milk as per phone instructions from the missus. But these days, trouble spills out from Donny's into the street around it like a bad odor and, as far as I can tell from my safe distance, the only folks who frequent Donny's are cold-blooded youths in athletic clothes, druggies, winos, and foul-mouthed women with Virginia Slims menthols bobbing in their mouths. All in all, the store and the block around seem as hard and hopeless as Death Row itself.

Standing in the street is a slick-headed kid in no shirt, boxer shorts visible above his oversized shorts pulled low on his hips, big shoes. He's talking to a woman who might be his mother or might not, with a huge derriere ballooning inside a pair of calf-high black and green stretch pants and a Dallas Cowboys t-shirt.

As we pull closer, she yells, "Ah mo kick yore ayess, bwoy! Ah mean it!" A crowd of onlookers has gathered outside to take in the action, squinting in the sun.

"Shee-it, bitch. Don't be talkin' that shit to *me* now! You only my aunt. You ain't my mother." Ruby rolls her eyes at me, but nobody's paying any attention to the silver Subaru wagon. From the corner, even in the air-conditioning, I can hear the boy's aunt yelling about calling cops and kicking asses.

"That was weird," I say.

"I thought we might be another drive-by story."

"Yeah, except we were the ones driving."

"Well, that's just the kind of twist they love on the news." This type of scene is the reason that Ruby never does the route alone. If

I'm not available, she gets someone else from the office to go with her.

We turn on Central Avenue, the main commercial thoroughfare in this part of town. The street has seen better days. Half the businesses are boarded up, and the ones that are left have a down-at-the-heels tiredness. There's a beauty parlor with a hand-painted picture of a woman in an afro on the plate glass, a dry cleaners with a faded sign hanging from a rusted post, a bar with no name were two men stand in a dark door, pool cues in their hands, watching us pass by, an auto repair shop with at least twenty cars in the lot that have not moved an inch since the Ford Administration.

Next stop—the Clancys—won't be so easy. I open the back door and take out the last meal. "Wish me luck," I say through clenched teeth.

"Good luck," says Ruby."

"One of these days, I'll let you take this one," I mutter after the door is shut.

I walk four houses down to the Clancys' while Ruby pulls past me and is waiting by the curb as I turn to go up the steps. I walk past the front house, a former crack joint where, in the early days of our route, we actually delivered meals to an old woman I half believed to be a hostage of a crowd of hard gangsters and their glassy-eyed vampire women who took the meals from me at the door each week without a word or glance. One day we arrived to find it boarded up and posted with orange no-trespassing-by-order-of-the-police signs, the former occupants no doubt taking their free meals at Huntsville nowadays.

I pass around the side of the front house and across the gravel yard, headed for the identical back house where the Clancys live.

The yard is lined with the remnants of several junked cars. On cue, as he does every week, the Clancys' homicidal dog lunges toward me from the shady underside of a rusted chassis beside the house. He's barking savagely, his lips curling up over the tops of his yellow gnarling teeth, the hair on his back bristling straight up. He makes it plain he'd rip my throat out if he had half a chance, but he hits the end of his chain and is jerked around so hard his skinny ass is thrown out front and he's barking at me backward. I desperately wish he would break his worthless neck. No doubt his life is harder than mine.

So too is Mrs. Clancy's. I think about how, two weeks ago in this same yard I stood waiting with the ridiculous meal in my hand while Mrs. Clancy loaded her daughter, a walking skeleton, into the back seat of a cab. The daughter, looking every bit like she'd just been liberated from a death camp, her teeth protruding past her lips, had already assumed the cadaver's mocking grin.

Today, though, no one is outside and I knock on the screen door.

"Who is it?"

"Meals on Wheels."

"Arright. Come on in."

I open the screen door. Mrs. Clancy is sitting on a sofa just inside the door.

"How you today?" she asks.

"Fine, just fine. I'll just leave this here," I say, depositing the tin plate on the end table beside the sofa. The interior is as dim as a grave, but I see that Mrs. Clancy is reading a book—the Bible. As I lean over to leave the meal on the table I see the word "LAMENTATIONS" across the top of the page. For some reason this causes me to look again at Mrs. Clancy, then retreat, muttering at her as I go, then scuttle out across the sun-cracked yard and down the steps to where Ruby waits in the car.

"How was the puppy today?" she asks.

"I survived."

"Are you hungry?"

"Starving."

"Where should we go?"

"Lou's." I say. "I need some barbecue."

"Okay, but I'm off meat."

"Really? Since when?"

"Oh, this weekend."

"Why?"

"I think red meat inhibits my yeast blockers."

"Your what?"

"My yeast blockers," says Ruby. "I wouldn't expect you to understand."

"And what is your basis for this idea?"

"It's just my idea. Is that all right with you?" Ruby's laughing like she knows this idea is stupid and she doesn't care. Half the time I think she makes this stuff up just to have a merry time yorking away at me, all the while casting me as every bit the smug idiot that I no doubt am. "Girls just wanna have fun." That's her motto while I fuss and fume away over the petty parameters of my job, my life, the friends I never see, the person I'll never be.

Ruby's set herself to giggling away at her own thoughts that are, I suppose, funny as a pegleg. But I can't escape the thought that the more of my dark ballast she throws off, the higher her balloon rises.

"Jeez, look at all those people outside Lou's," says Ruby.

She's right: there's a crowd outside the restaurant and the street is full of cars, including a camera truck from a local TV station. My first thought is panic: the place has been held up, the site of grisly murder. Or a repeat of the atrocity of several years ago when an off-duty cop put a neighborhood kid in a strangle-hold when he thought he saw a gun. The kid died of a broken neck and no gun was ever found.

But no, there's no ambulance and the crowd on the street is mostly men and women in business clothes, not the usual crime-scene thrill-seekers. We park over a block away and walk back. We squeeze our way in the door and find ourselves face to face with none other than the mayor herself.

She's a stout fireplug of a trooper with a mannish suit, frozen crooked smile, and a helmet of frosted hair. She's surrounded by people and cameras and when her eyes fall on us she says, "Ha dee, y'all! Y'all doon all right?"

I feel the cameras swivel toward me, the lights shining in my eyes. "Just stopped in for some barbecue," I say idiotically. Her Honor is grinning like a wolf now and I think for a moment she might actually eat me herself.

"Well, arrightie, then. Come on in and gitch'all some. This here's the best dang food in the world!" All at once the mayor's attention and the cameras swing on to something else. There are so many people I can't see the counter. Come to think of it, I can't even smell the food.

Before I know it, we're out of there trudging back to the car.

"She's a lot fatter than I thought," says Ruby.

"Well, damn. What do you want to do now?"

"Oh, I guess we'd better head back to work. We're about out of time."

Great. I'm starving now, hot and thoroughly out of sorts at the prospect of skipping lunch. But I keep quiet. I'm weary of my complaints.

Ruby sails up the street on the waft of her big skirt. In the next block a group of men in a grassless yard stop talking to watch us. Ruby is already in the front seat turning over the engine as I walk up. Suddenly she seems anxious to be done with me and back at her desk answering the phone and mucking around with her spreadsheets. Except there's a problem. The car won't start.

"Oh, great!" she says. "What the fuck are we gonna do now?"

"Try it again," I say. "It'll start this time."

She does and it doesn't.

"You have triple-A, right?"

Ruby is already digging in her fanny pack for her phone. "Where is my phone? Dang, I must have left it at the office."

"Well, that's too bad, because I always leave mine at the office when I go out to lunch."

Ruby looks at me in disblief. "You're kidding."

"I wish I were." I look up the street to where the mayor's entourage is moving out onto Central Avenue outside Lou's. I have half a mind to march back down and cadge a ride from some office aide or maybe even sweetheart herself. I look the other way and see that the guys in the front yard have taken a more active interest in us and started edging down the street our way.

"Come on," I say, opening my door. "Let's go find a phone."

"Where?" Ruby asks.

"At Lou's. Come on."

Finally she climbs out, sighing like a bellows. The gents from up the street approach our car, spreading out as the come.

"Hey!" says one. "Y'all need some help?"

"No," I say. "We're fine."

"Y'all stay 'roun' here?"

"Car trouble? My cousin's a mechanic. I could call him for you."

"No, thanks. We're okay. Car's okay."

"Hey, where y'all goin' so fas'?"

"Back up to Lou's—see if the crowd's all gone."

"Hey, listen here," says one of the men, breaking a smile. "Tell that white bitch get her fat ass out the Easside. She don't belong here." The other men start laughing. They stop edging toward us.

"I sure will," I say. Ruby's walked a few steps farther on.

"Y'all don't worry. We'll keep an eye on your car."

"Great," I say. "I appreciate it."

I feel Ruby staring at me, but I decide to keep my own counsel to the corner where the crowd at Lou's seems thicker and rowdier than before. The TV crew is loading up their van. The mayor is nowhere in sight.

"Can't use the phone here."

"I suppose not," says Ruby.

"Let's walk up to Mrs. Clancy's. We'll call triple-A from there."

"You think it's okay?"

"Sure, why not?"

"Well, okay. . . If you think so." Ruby casts a last look down toward her car.

"I do," I say. "Let's go."

We push back through the crowd in front of Lou's and back up Central one block to the Clancy's. The houses on Central sit up high to catch the breeze. Some are fine older houses, well-tended with broad porches and swings. Others are smaller shacks with busted screen doors, bare foundations, and hard dirt yards. The equatorial sun is hot enough to slow the traffic as it crests the hill. Every driver stares at us.

"This is great," says Ruby. "Just what I needed."

"Why?" I say. "What's so bad about your life, huh?"

"Oh, what would you know? You're so wrapped up in yourself."

"Oh, really? So try me."

"Well, they moved my father to a rest home because he had another stroke and I can't afford the airfare to go up there, my car's broken down, and Jeff broke up with me this weekend."

I stop walking. "Chuck?"

"Oh, will you stop. There is no Chuck. His name is Jeff."

"The repo man?"

"Yeah. I guess he repossessed his affections. Or something like that." Ruby tries to laugh, but coughs instead. We start walking again.

"Jeez, I'm sorry."

"It's okay."

"Is there anything I can do for you?"

Ruby looks at me with a weak smile. "No. I don't think there is anything you can do for me." I think for a moment she might be crying, but I'm not sure. Then we're there, in front of the shotgun shack that's in front of the shotgun shack where the Clancys live.

"They've got an evil dog," I say.

"So I've heard."

Up the steps, around the front house, and we're crossing the Clancy's dirt yard. The dog sticks his nose out from under the car. I brace for the attack, but the next minute the mongrel has trotted out in a tail-wagging, head-bent, chop-licking saunter and sidled his filthy snout right into Ruby's waiting hands. She rubs him all over his head, behind the ears, and down his back. His ears are bent way back and his face wears the look of pure rapture. Ruby sweet-talks the hound into the dirt where he rolls onto his back and offers his stomach for scratching.

"Oh, man!" I say. "How did you do that?"

"Voodoo," says Ruby.

I knock on Mrs. Clancy's door.

"Who is it?" she asks.

"It's the Meals on Wheels folks, Mrs. Clancy."

"Ah hah," she sighs, making her way to the door. She pushes open the screen door and nods at me, her eyes moving from me to Ruby to me again. She seems confused, but in no way frightened to find us standing on her porch.

"Mrs. Clancy, this is my partner, Ruby. Our car broke down up the street. Could we use your phone to call the tow truck?"

I watch as the reservations disappear and Mrs. Clancy smiles. "Why yes, baby. Y'all come on in here. Phone's right yonder."

We step inside where it's dim but cool, a box fan blowing from down the unlit hall. Ruby sits down on the end of the sofa and rifles through her bag for the number. Mrs. Clancy sits at the end of the sofa. The TV is turned on and tuned to a soap opera. The Bible is closed and resting on top of the set. Ruby dials a number and waits.

"My husband's gone out now or I'd have him drive you," Mrs. Clancy offers tiredly.

"That's okay," I say as Ruby explains about the car to someone on the other end. "Ruby's got triple-A."

"Triple *who*?"

"It's like insurance. So if you need it they tow your car for free."

"Is that right," she says, watching the TV.

Ruby hangs up. "They're coming."

"Well, that's good," says Mrs. Clancy. She's gone back to her soap opera. On cue my stomach lets rip with a thundering growl. This snaps Mrs. C. back to attention.

"I bet y'all're hungry."

"Oh, no," I say. "We—"

"Are you hungry, miss?" she asks Ruby.

"Starving," says Ruby.

"Well, arright then," says Mrs. Clancy, a big grin spreading over her face. She jumps up from the sofa and disappears down the hall.

"What are we gonna do?" I say. The last thing I want to do is have one of our clients feed us.

"Eat," says Ruby.

"What?" I say.

"That," says Ruby, nodding to the tin pie pan and the blue cold bag sitting on the marble side table right where I left it twenty minutes ago. And she's right too, because that minute Mrs. Clancy has reappeared with two small china plates and two forks. She opens the meal and scoops a tiny bit of meat, carrots and a half a canned pear onto each plate.

"That's all right," she says. "I got mines from yesterday still. I done ate at my sister's so I saved it. But y'all're in a hurry and I got all the time in the world to reheat that one from yesterday."

"We tried to eat at Lou's," says Ruby, taking a plate. "Did you ever eat there?"

"Lord, yes," says Mrs. C. "Fact is, I used to be one of Lou's best customers. Now the doctor says I can't eat that greasy food no more. Sometimes I wonder what good it is to even be alive if a body can't have a good sausage sandwich now and then."

"You probably could," says Ruby. "Once in a while."

"Oh, child, do you really b'lieve that?"

Ruby nods. "Yeah, I do."

Mrs. Clancy smiles as wide as a planet. Ruby smiles at Mrs. Clancy, then turns the smile my way, saying, "You should try it. It's pretty good."

Slowly I raise the fork to my mouth and eat. The taste of the gravy and meat are overpoweringly rich.

"You're right," I say. "It's good." And it *is* good. Really good. At this moment, in fact, it occurs to me that this may be the very best thing that I have ever eaten

The Loneliness of Marriage

Jackson heard the voices in the street before he was awake. They produced in his dreams images of swarming, murderous mobs, their grimed faces angry in the torchlight. In a single motion, he swung his feet out of bed onto the hardwood floor and grabbed the broom handle from where it stood behind the doorjamb. He stepped carefully to the window and looked down into the street. A group of noisy teenaged boys sauntered down the middle of the street. The streetlamp threw their lengthening shadows from midblock to the corner. There were only four of them, but their voices echoed so loudly in the quiet air that Jackson counted them again.

He watched them until they turned the corner from Willow onto Bergenhurst Avenue. After they were gone, Jackson leaned on the windowsill and looked up and down his street at the houses of his neighbors, most of whom he did not know. The houses were stout, solid, nearly identical and so close together that you could almost reach out from the window of one and touch the next. Cars were parked along the street and Jackson made a mental note to remember that tomorrow was sweeper day. He'd have to put his wife's car in the driveway if she weren't awake when he left for the train.

He moved back into the dark room. He put the broom handle back in its place behind the door. He leaned across the bed on one elbow and watched his wife where she lay. The shadows in the room seemed to gather around her, to protect her. Jackson could hear her breathe. He pressed close to her face to listen. He ran his hand down the soft curve of her back to where her body flared out below her waist and slipped his hand into the warmth between her legs. She mumbled something he could not understand and squirmed to push his hand away. He stepped again onto the floor of the room.

Jackson walked down the creaking stairs to the living room, admiring as he always did the solid workmanship of his house: the inlaid wood around the base of the newel post at the foot of the stairs, the stained glass window above the tiled foyer. He walked toward the kitchen, which lay at the back of the house. Without bothering to turn on the lights, he opened a cupboard and took out a glass. He opened one of the small doors in the cabinet over the refrigerator and took out a bottle of bourbon. Good southern drink, thought Jackson, fuck this blasted northern affectation of scotch or, worse, some Italianate liquor in one of those outlandishly necked and pebbled bottles.

He poured some into a glass and drank it without ice or water.

Then he poured another and put the cap back on the bottle. He walked into the living room and stood beside the window looking at the house next door. The light was on in one of the downstairs rooms. There were no curtains on the windows and a dining table and a glassed credenza were visible in the room. He stood silently in the living room sipping his bourbon from the heavy, leaded glass until a woman stepped into the frame of the lighted window. She was thin and drawn, but younger than Jackson and attractive in a somber way. She peered through the window toward Jackson, but with the lights on in the room, she could only have been looking at her reflection in a black pane of glass.

After a moment she moved out of sight. Jackson finished his drink and went back into the kitchen. He unscrewed the cap and had lifted the bottle to pour when the phone rang. Jackson put down the bottle and picked up the receiver before it rang again.

"Hello," he said.

"I knew you were watching."

Jackson laughed quietly, without humor. "Come over," he said.

"I can't," said the woman. "Not this time."

"You could," suggested Jackson.

"Yes. I guess I could."

"But you won't."

"No," she said.

"Then why did you call?"

"I'm not sure," she said.

"Then to hell with you," said Jackson. He heard her speak his name once as though in miniature as he hung the receiver in its cradle on the wall. He picked up the bottle and poured another drink. When he had finished, he rinsed the glass and put it in the drainer and reached the bottle back into the cabinet over the refrigerator. As he moved toward the stairs, he turned to look at the window next door. It was dark.

His wife slept on in the shadows of their room, tangled in the difficult sheets. Jackson lay beside her in the bed they had shared for over ten years, cursing his wakefulness. After several minutes, he whispered,

"Do you remember the first house we lived in after we were married?" He paused as though waiting for an answer, but he knew none was coming. "We always kept a row of tomatoes on the sill in the kitchen window and the neighbors were forever coming around and pestering us when all we wanted was to be left to ourselves. The yard was big and grassy and there were Canada geese in the summer and deer in the winter and we looked for the first redwing blackbird that told us spring was on the way. I loved walking up the country roads out there past meadows full of cowshit and wildflowers. And remember how we played like children in the snow in the winter? It was still a novelty then. Like everything else."

Jackson stopped talking. He lay thinking for a long time until the unfaltering evenness of his wife's breathing finally lulled him into a black and dreamless sleep.

Sue and Frank

"What do you mean you lost your wedding ring?" said Sue Davidson to her husband Frank who sat in the passenger seat of their car, which idled beside the arrivals curb at Terminal B of Newark Airport. Two minutes before, Frank had emerged from the sliding doors, tossed his tidy suit bag into the backseat of their Accord, piled into the front and announced without so much as a prologue that he had lost his wedding ring somewhere in Washington, D.C., sometime during the last four days. Now he sat looking across at his wife, the thin angular lines of his face heightened by the crisp folds of his London Fog raincoat. The bustle and excitement of travel that he brought into the car was at odds with Sue's mood.

"Yeah, it was the damnedest thing. Right in the middle of my big meeting with Thompson, I looked down and it was gone." He held his left hand up, fingers outstretched in a number five gesture. Sure enough, there was no ring, though Sue fancied she could make out the indentation in the skin of his finger as though he had just taken it off.

"I can't believe it!" she said.

"Well, you don't have to look like that. I didn't *mean* to lose it." Frank had adopted the managerial tone of voice he had acquired after years of supervising large office staffs.

"It's just that, well, I just can't believe you didn't notice something."

"Honey, do you, ah, think we could get going? I'm kind of tired and I'd like a shower before bed."

Sue jammed the gearshift into drive and lurched away from the curb. Instinctively, Frank glanced over his left shoulder to check the traffic. Fine, thought Sue, he goes away for four days on one of his business trips which, by the way, seemed to be getting more frequent all the time, and now he was going to shower for thirty minutes and then pile into bed with a report or some fat slick trade magazine. No doubt about it, an hour after they hit home he'd be snoring away. Never mind what she might want once in a while.

"Strange as it sounds," he said, "I didn't notice it until I was in that meeting with Thompson. I said, 'Jesus, I've lost my wedding ring!' and she said—

"She?" said Sue.

"Yeah. Thompson. Janet Thompson from our Washington office. I'm sure I've told you about her before."

"Oh, well," she muttered. "I guess you did." Big fluffy snowflakes had started to fall, turning to water the instant they hit the windshield, just in time to be swept away by the wipers. Sue felt her mind become clouded and jumbled.   Her emotions swarmed and crowded together like an angry, volatile mob. Certainly she felt no jealousy about Frank's meeting with this Thompson (was it some new business convention to refer to female colleagues by their last names?   It sounded so efficient and powerful), he worked with women everyday.   No, what really galled her was the thought of this other woman, well-dressed, confident, successful, knowing something intimate about their marriage while Sue whistled away in her fool's paradise. She could just imagine the show of sympathy and concern this hard-nosed, corporate-climbing career woman had displayed while to herself she laughed at the pathetic wife off somewhere blissfully ignorant, powerless, forgotten.

Frank kept on blathering. "She said, 'Well, you have to find it, that's all there is to it.'"

"How kind of her," said Sue.

"I thought so," said Frank.

"So we got the check right away and—"

"What, were you at lunch?"

"Dinner," said Frank. "And I went straight back to my room and searched high and low. I even went back to the bar where I had stopped for a cocktail that evening and also the hotel restaurant. Nada. Of course, my room had been cleaned by then. I figured if housekeeping had gotten hold of it, good luck ever seeing that ring again."

Good old Frank, thought Sue. When his pal Stan—Stosh—got caught cheating the IRS big-time and went to that country club prison in upstate New York, Frank had been really pissed off. But when it came to hired help, they were not to be trusted. To hear

Frank go on, you'd think the blue collars of the world were just waiting to steal the dirt out from under your fingernails, though there'd be slim pickings from Frank in that department.

"So that's it?" said Sue as they pulled onto the northbound Turnpike. The snow was coming down harder and cars had begun to slow down. The landscape had begun to take on a steely grey aspect, the mirrorlike slickness of the pavement reflecting the red taillights of thousands of commuters headed home.

"What else can I say, honey? You know how much that ring meant to me. I wouldn't have lost it for the world."

He had dropped the managerial tone now and fallen back on his old standby Mr. Charm voice that he had always used to such advantage, especially with Sue. But she wasn't buying it now.

"But you did lose it. I just can't believe it."

"What do you want me to do?" said Frank. "I'm sorry, okay? I lost the ring. I didn't *want* to lose it. It just happened. I'll get another, I promise."

Case closed. Debit recorded in the unrecoverable loss column. Dead letter file. Sue opened her mouth, then closed it again. What more could she say?

"Good thing we'll be home before the snow gets bad," said Frank with forced cheerfulness. "I hate to drive in the snow."

"You're not driving, Frank. I am." They rode in silence the rest of the way home.

Lately, Sue had acquired the habit of waking in the middle of the night and wandering around the house poking into this and that, doing nothing in particular. She told herself that she delighted in the pleasant perversity of being awake when the rest of the world slept, but the truth was she felt more comfortable and secure in the wee hours. Sue found herself increasingly overwhelmed with the small things in life. She felt that she literally had to hold on for dear life as Earth itself careened through space. When the world was quiet and still and asleep, at those times and those times alone, Sue felt like she was in control of something, that the progress of time was slowed down to a speed she could manage.

Also, the big modern house that Frank had insisted on buying over her objections seemed cold to the point of being alien during the day. (She would have preferred something more Victorian that she could decorate with baskets of potpourri, stencilled wallpaper and lots of duck decoys and antiques.) But at night the house seemed softer and more comfortable.

She poured a glass of red wine and wandered into the study and looked until she found the photo album that had the pictures of their wedding. She took this into the living room, set her wine on the glass coffee table and burrowed down into the deep cushions of their sectional sofa.

Had it been ten years already? Of course, she had gained some weight. How could she not? Sitting around the house all day. Oh well, she kept busy enough between volunteering at the library, church activities, and with her friends. But there was no real need to work. Frank had discouraged it, in fact, not because he didn't feel it was proper, but because it screwed up their income tax bracket or something.

She never had thought she would be a housewife. She had always dreaded the thought of it. When she met Frank she had just gone back to school to work on a masters in psychology, but she never finished. Before that she worked at a number of odd jobs that never amounted to anything.

She found herself wishing idly for children, but the day for that had also come and gone. She married Frank when she was in her early thirties. There was still time then, and they talked about it often, but the time never seemed to be right and year had followed year and here she was in her early forties. Technically, she could still consider the possibility, but in truth, the idea had stopped appealing to her the way it once had. If things seemed this complicated without kids, what would it be like with? Anyway, she didn't want to be sixty with a child in high school.

As she stared one-by-one at the pictures, a thought began to present itself in her mind. Not a new thought to her, but expressed with more clarity and force than before: It wasn't supposed to be this way. She had agreed to a different set of conditions fifteen years before. She had signed on to a different agenda. Frank was a business major who was going to make enough to keep them fed and spend the rest of his time playing bass with a New Wave band that he and his friends kept trying to start. That dream lasted exactly one month and one gig and then fell to pieces when Interworld called and recruited him straight from college.

"Still up?" said Frank from the hall door. He stood in his pajamas and robe, well-dressed in the middle of the night. He squinted into the lighted room, his eyes adjusting to the light.

"Up again," Sue answered. She took a sip of the wine. The glass was cold against her lips, but the wine felt round and warm as it rolled across her tongue. She expected Frank would turn and go back to bed, but instead he crossed the white pile carpet and settled beside her on the sofa. Why did he seem to be growing thinner over the years as she grew more plump? The question mystified more than annoyed her.

"I'm sorry about the ring," he said.

"Oh, it's okay. I made too much of it."

"No, you didn't. It was stupid of me."

"Let's not talk about it anymore," she said. After a moment she said, "Frank?"

"Hmmm?"

"Let's get in the car and drive."

"Where? Where do you want to go?"

"Nowhere in particular. Everywhere. Don't you remember when we used to talk about driving across the country? Let's do it now. We could go down south—I've never been down there. It's slower and calmer down there, I think.   We won't take any interstates, just country roads. We'll stop at every general store and main street diner we come to. We'll buzz into each town, buy postcards and buzz out. We'll stay in tacky tourist courts and stop at all the historical markers. We'll go to McDonald's and buy two coffees, fill up the thermos and then get refills for the road."

Sue became animated as she talked, but Frank just forced a thin half-smile and said, "You're kidding, right?"

"No," said Sue, shaking her head, "I'm not."

"But honey. I have a job. I couldn't just walk out. I have appointments. I have at least ten clients coming in this week. I'd love to take a vacation. Really. How about next summer? I'll put in a leave request now. But not on the spur of the moment."

Sue nodded and took another sip of her wine. For no good reason, she felt a sudden and overwhelming urge to ask her husband if he had slept with anyone else since they were married.

She fought down the urge. Partly because she had made a promise to herself years before that she would never ask. Partly because she knew the answer would depress her no matter what it was. But mostly she realized that to even want to ask the question at all meant that some profound circumstance had changed in a way that made the answer irrelevant.

She nodded again and said, "Yeah, maybe in the summer. It's too cold now anyway."

The next morning, after Sue had dropped Frank at the station to join the other commuters who stood hunched in their long, thick clothes on the platform, their breath turning into tiny clouds in the frozen air, she went home and packed an overnight bag.

She made a pot of coffee and took it to the kitchen table. She gathered up paper and a pen and sat at the table under the heart carved in a highbacked, Dutch style bench, the most old-fashioned furnishing in the house and her favorite place to sit. She drank coffee and wrote a note to Frank. She wrote that she was leaving and taking the car. He'd get along without it and seldom drove it anyway. She also wrote that she would probably be back, though as she did she wondered if this were true.

She reread the note. It didn't express her feelings, but it would do. She had a second cup of coffee and wondered vaguely where she would spend the night. She didn't have much cash, but plenty of credit cards and that would hold her for a while.

She stood, rinsed her cup and put it in the drainer. She put the note on the countertop and gathered up all her bulky winter clothes that she liked so much because they were comforting and because they hid her figure. She took her old sleeping bag, too. She hadn't used it in years, but you never know when you might need a sleeping bag.

As she pulled the front door to, she saw that the mailman had been by already. Compulsively, she took the mail from the box and looked to see if anything had come for her. There was a Land's End catalog, another from Victoria's Secret (Frank had even stopped enjoying those), a bill from New Jersey Bell, a fat envelope of coupons, and a small, oddly bulky envelope from the hotel where Frank had stayed in Washington.

She didn't have to open the envelope to know what was inside. She could even feel the outline of the ring through the paper. She stood for several minutes holding the envelope, letting the significance of it flood over her. She considered her choices. The fact of the envelope and her absolute control of it filled her with an excitement that seemed out of proportion to its importance.

Finally, she jammed the envelope into the pocket of her coat. She stuffed the rest of the mail back into the mailbox and turned to lock the front door. She walked carefully down the front steps and out to the car. The snow continued to fall and she noticed where her earlier footsteps had already been filled in by a new carpet of flakes. Pretty soon they would be invisible, as though she had never walked there at all.

She threw her things in a messy heap in the backseat and set out for the highway. She felt good as she thought about the ring in her pocket and the security it gave her, like a tiny golden life raft.

Bourgeois Home Cooking and Bar-B-Q

The name of the place was the "Bourgeois Home Cooking and Bar-B-Q." At least those were the words hand-painted on the side of the trailer in a primitive assortment of colors, sizes, and upper- and lower-case letters.

The trailer was the ordinary, two-wheel recreational variety though it seemed to have been retired from the road long ago. Its hitch rested on a stack of cinder blocks, its tires were flat and cracked, and the whole rig teetered precariously in the mud and tall weeds along Route 9, outside the town of Goodfellow, deep in the piney woods of East Texas. A cloud of smoke rose from a red-brick barbecue pit behind the trailer. The aroma of cooked meat must have been a source of perpetual torment for any dog within a mile.

"Did you see that place?" Maxine asked her husband Ray.

"Yep, I guess we'd better stop," he said in a bored tone.

"Well, we don't *have* to go," said Maxine.

"No," said Ray. "I want to." He swung the Lincoln off the blacktop and onto the gravel shoulder, set his left turn signal and checked his rear view mirror.

"You don't sound like you want to."

"Listen," Ray barked. "Don't start with me."

"Okay, okay," said Maxine, throwing her hands in the air. Ray swung the car around in a wide U-turn that took him to the opposite shoulder. He rolled to a stop thirty feet from the trailer.

Like most roadside objects, the Bourgeois looked different close up than it had whizzing by at sixty. Details were clearer: a tiny window with sliding glass, an awning strung from makeshift poles over the door, a tiny orange and red sticker in the window that said, "Catalunya."

Then there was the yard beyond: a shack of weathered grey wood, ancient rusted farm machinery surrounded by weeds as tall as a person, and white chickens that clucked and pecked around the yard, their jerking eyes filled with terror. The incessant rasp of cicadas seemed to expand as it rose through the trees and filled the hot air.

Maxine and Ray stood on the gravel shoulder. Their doors made a substantial "thunk thunk" sound that caused a small face to appear in the frame of the decrepit screen door. She was at least seventy and could not have stood more than four feet ten or eleven. Her skin was drawn and brown like a tanned hide or the skin of a shrunken head, but the screen door softened her features which were fine and precise.

Ray and Maxine exchanged glances. This was their kind of place. They had spent the better part of the decade of their marriage tracking down this very type of funky, eccentric dive. They had eaten in restaurants shaped like donuts, ducks and dinosaurs. They had stayed in concrete teepee motels in Arizona, little Alamos outside San Antonio, and cabooses in goofy roadside attractions, motels and eateries had been their thing, their inside joke. They even had an expression for their pastime that was as private as sex and almost as powerful: "Another Ray and Max adventure."

But that was all over now.

They followed the old woman inside. The interior, though impossibly crowded—no bigger than ten by twenty feet—managed to accommodate not only a small, griddle-topped propane-fueled cook stove, but also a tiny Formica-covered dining table with metal legs and matching blue metal folding chairs. Cool air circulated inside the dark interior by way of two fans set in the window and on top of the counter between the kitchen and dining area.

At second glance, the proprietor seemed to grow younger. She wore a loosely fitting housedress in an extravagant floral print, a fringed apron and a pair of gold lamé sultan slippers curled up at the toes. Her bony body seemed to move independently inside her jumper. The door slammed noisily behind her. Ray and Maxine pulled chairs out from the table and sat. The old lady stood before them, arms akimbo.

"I'm glad you folks stopped," she said. "I ain't had a single damn customer all day."

Maxine chucked self-consciously. Ray had begun to read the fly-speckled plastic Hires root beer menu that sat propped precariously on top of the tiny Coldspot refrigerator. He took off his sunglasses and put them on the table where they lay with a slick hardness that Maxine found embarrassingly out of place in this funky old dive.

"What can I get for you folks to drink? I got some cold RC colas. Big Red? Or can I put on some ice tea for you?"

"The RC sounds good," said Ray.

"Me too," said Maxine.

The woman nodded. Maxine and Ray watched as she opened the fridge, took out the bottles one at a time and set them on the counter. She removed the caps with an opener she pulled from a two-pound French Market coffee can full of kitchen implements. Before bringing them to the table, she wrapped napkins around both bottles. She moved with all the ritual formality of a Japanese tea service. Maxine and Ray followed her movements with rapt attention.

"Barbecue?" Ray asked.

"Sir, I have got the best damn barbecue in Anderson County."

"I bet you do," said Ray, grinning. "Okay, then, I'll try the beef plate."

"Pickles and onions?"

"Sure."

"And you, ma'am?"

"I'll have the same," said Maxine.

Okay, folks. It'll be just a minute," said the old woman. She took a lidless pressure cooker from where it sat on the stove and went outside. The screen door slammed behind her.

"Whoa," said Ray. "Cool place."

"*Really* cool," said Maxine.

"Another Max and Ray adven—" Ray stopped abruptly. Maxine jerked her head and glared at him.

"Don't say that," she said.

"Say what?"

"You know what."

"No, I don't know what," said Ray, his voice rising.

"Our old routine. I know what you're up to. You want to make me nostalgic. Make me change my mind. Just forget it, Ray. I agreed to come on this little trip with you as long as it stayed nice and simple. One last jaunt for old time's sake. That's it. When we get back to—"

She broke off as the door yanked open and the old woman came inside with a side of brisket hanging out over the rim of the pressure cooker. The trailer filled at once with the smell of cooked meat. Right on cue, Maxine and Ray started salivating like Pavlov's dogs.

"Where you folks from?" asked the woman as she stuck a meat fork into the brisket and hauled it onto the cutting board.

"Austin," said Maxine. Ray nodded.

"Austin, is it? I ain't been to Austin for many years. Actually I ain't been anywhere but over to Tyler a couple of times in the last fifteen years. That was when my husband Pete died. He and I travelled quite a bit. After he passed away it just wasn't the same. Sure like Austin, though. Love to go back someday."

She cut several steaming slices of the meat and arranged them on Chinet plates complete with the customary complements: pickles, onion slices, steamy pinto beans and an ice-cream scoopful of mustardy potato salad.

"My name's Ruth Dalton," she said. "What's y'alls'?"

"Maxine. And this is my—" she paused slightly. Ruth glanced up from her work with the plates. "My husband Ray."

Ruth brought the plates to the table and set them before the diners.

"Boy that looks good," said Ray, setting aside the obligatory slice of white sandwich bread that sat perched atop the plates.

"Y'all mind if I sit with you?"

"Not at all, "said Maxine, exchanging a glance with Ray as Ruth settled herself. Maxine knew this was the kind of thing that Ray loved. Getting to know people they met on their travels. In that way, Ray hadn't changed a hair since college. It wasn't enough for him to just drive through a place. He had to get to know it. Eat the food, meet the people, read historical markers in front of the courthouse and sit around drinking coffee in all the local haunts. They never covered much ground on their trips, but then, that had been part of the charm.

"So why do you call this place the 'Bourgeois'?" said Ray, jamming a forkful of brisket in his mouth. "Seems like an unusual name."

Ruth smiled and said, "That's a long story. A good story, but a long one. I'll tell you if I can smoke while I tell it."

Ray shrugged at Maxine who shrugged back. "Sure," said Ray. Ruth pulled a pack of Doral 100s from her apron pocket. She dug one of the cigarettes out of the red and white package and lit it with a kitchen match she scritched on the edge of the table.

"My husband Pete was a communist," said Ruth. She tilted her head slightly and looked sideways through a cloud of smoke around her head. She seemed to wait for the shock of that statement to sink in, but when Ray and Maxine kept on eating, she said, "Well, I always said he was, but to tell the truth, no one who ever came from East Texas was an honest-to-God communist. But he was the most interesting man I ever met. He left home during the Depression when he was only sixteen. He rode the rails all over the country. Somewhere along the way he met a guy named Cantú. This Cantú was a socialist and a union organizer. The kind we all used to call Reds. Anyway, Cantú was the one who got Pete all interested in communism. Cantú told Pete that he was on his way to Spain to fight in their Civil War that was starting up over there. Pete didn't know a dang thing about Spain, but he didn't have anything better to do so he went along with Cantú.

"Your husband was in the Abraham Lincoln Brigade?" Ray asked, amazed.

"You heard of that, eh?"

"Heard about it?" said Ray. "It's famous. Legendary."

Ruth nodded. "Mister, you'd be surprised at all the things the folks in Goodfellow never heard about. So anyway, Pete and this Cantú fellow went and fought in that Spanish Civil War. Cantú got himself killed, but Pete came back okay and with a whole lot of stories to tell. He met a bunch of famous writers and people while he was there. People who wrote letters to him until he died or they died, whichever. He always felt like that was the high point of his life and everything else was downhill after that. He went into the Army for a year or two. After that, he came back to Goodfellow and got a veteran's loan and started a place called 'Pete's' in town. It wasn't much, just a greasy spoon, but it was his place and everybody went there.

"Now Pete never made any secrets about his politics and he'd argue with anyone about workers' rights or fascism or whatever.

Most folks liked Pete and accepted him for what he was. But along the line he must've made someone real mad because one night they came and burned out the place. Cops said they didn't have a clue, but he always said they were lying. May even have been them. He was probably right. Everybody knew Pete hated the cops worst of all.

"That happened way back in 1947. We were just courting then, but when he had the fire, he seemed to need me, so I went on and married him. My parents were quite upset about that and I guess they never forgave me. But I figure when you find your right person, you get with them and stay with them."

Ray and Maxine exchanged glances over their food.

"Well, when Pete got paid off by the insurance company, he moved out here and started this place and saved a nice nest egg besides. But he hated the town more than ever. Said they were nothing but a bunch of damn Bourgeois and there ain't nothing worse than the damn Bourgeoisie. I said well, if it weren't for them Bourgeois you wouldn't have money to start this new place. He thought that was funny as a crutch so he decided he would call this new place the Bourgeois. Thing was, most of these East Texas rednecks around here are about as dumb as a shovel and they had no idea what that word meant. They thought it was just Pete putting on Frenchy airs. So they came anyway. And they been coming ever since."

"That's a hell of a story," said Ray.

"He sounds like an amazing man," said Maxine wistfully.

"When I met Pete, I was just East Texas white trash. But I became something else because of him. Learned about things I never would have known about, been to places I never would've gone. In '66 they had a thirtieth reunion of the Lincoln Brigade in Barcelona, Spain. We went over for that. Went to New York, too. There was Pete with all these old men in berets talking about the war. Some of them were famous, Pete said. He told me their names, but I forgot them all.

"So here I am, stuck running Pete's restaurant. No way to get out of it. Y'all got the right idea out on a vacation driving around. I'd leave this old place in a minute if I could figure out how to do it. Well, now I told you all about me, you go on and tell me about yourselves."

"Us?" Ray asked, turning the tines of plastic fork toward himself.

"Yeah, sure," said Ruth, tapping out another cigarette.

"There isn't much interesting to say about us," said Ray.

"Well, I figure whenever two people whose marriage is on the rocks are out driving around together in the middle of the week a couple of hundred miles from home, there's got to be some kind of story to tell."

Maxine imagined that she could actually hear the muscles in Ray's jaw tighten.

"'Nother RC?" asked Ruth, waving a nicotine-stained finger at the empties.

"Now you wait a minute," said Ray, finally able to speak. "What makes you think you can—"

"Aw calm down, young man," said Ruth. "You don't need to get all huffy. I was just making conversation. I see y'all come in here with your long faces. I think, this is a husband and wife on the skids. Been together a while, too. Long enough not to have to keep up a chatter all the damn time. Hell, my Pete and me didn't hardly say anything to each other the last ten years. Didn't need to. Married people get to a point where talk don't matter anymore. That's where you are. I know it."

She paused. Ray and Maxine had forgotten their food. They sat staring at this mad leprechaun of an old woman.

"Except something's come up. I'd bet the Bourgeois I know what it is."

Ray scowled and looked down at his plate though his appetite had completely vanished.

"I'm right, too, ain't I, Maxine? I don't want to pry none. I just want to know if I'm right." She looked like she was about break into a little jig. "Ain't it always the same damn thing?"

Ray squirmed uncomfortably, but Ruth ignored him.

"But how did you know?" said Maxine.

"Honey, everybody might have a different story, but you'd be surprised how dang similar they are sometimes."

Maxine smiled. She was starting to enjoy this crazy woman. She said, "I believe I'll take that RC now, please."

Ruth stood and went to the refrigerator and returned with another napkin swaddled bottle. She set it in front of Maxine and took the empty away.

Suddenly Ray blurted out, "Don't I get a chance?"

Ruth stopped moving and stared at him.

"I mean, I guess it doesn't matter if you love your wife faithfully for years and do right by her all that time. You step over the line one time—just once—and it's all over. It's like nothing good ever happened. None of it counts. Is that it?"

"Son you—" began Ruth.

But Maxine said, "No, Ray, that was what you never understood. You thought everything was so great all those years. You thought I really enjoyed watching you chase up the career ladder, brown-nosing people you hated just to get something you never wanted anyway."

Ray looked at his wife with tired eyes. "You never said a word about that stuff."

"I did, Ray. Plenty of times. You never heard me. You never wanted to hear. The thing with Cherise was just the last straw. Things had been wrong for years."

"But we had fun. All our travels. All those great trips we had. Our adventures. I always made time for that and I thought you really enjoyed them, too."

"I did. At first. When it was just you and me and nothing between us. When you belonged to me and not to your company. Later, when everything started coming apart, I realized we weren't travelling anymore, we were running. Running to keep from facing our lives."

Ray stared at Maxine, then let his eyes sink down. The couple had forgotten Ruth, forgotten that they were in a trailer on the side of the road in deep East Texas, full of brisket and RC Cola. Ruth laid a tiny lime-green check next to Ray's plate. As she moved away, Maxine watched Ray look up at Ruth, like the medieval paintings of martyrs rolling their eyes toward heaven.

He glanced at the check and took out a ten dollar bill. Maxine heard him whisper, "Jeez, that's cheap." Same old Ray, she thought. Never too upset not to recognize a good deal. She thought about a psychologist she had seen once on Oprah who said you can't change people you love. All you can do is decide if they're worth the hassle the way they are. She watched as Ray handed the bill and the check back to Ruth and said, "Keep it."

"Thank you," she said.

Ray and Maxine stood and started to leave. The feeling of unfinished business hung heavily in the close space of the trailer. Each of the three had, in their way, given up something of themselves to one another without the satisfaction of a receipt-in-kind. And as much as any of them felt the other had something they wanted, lunch was over and the road was calling.

"Well, it was a pleasure to meet you," said Ruth.

"Sure. Likewise," said Ray.

"If you're ever in Austin. . ." said Maxine.

"I'd love to," said Ruth, but no one moved to give an address.

"Bye," said Ray.

"Bye, now," said Ruth, watching them step down from the Bourgeois. "Y'all take care now."

Maxine followed Ray down the ditch and back up to their car. The blinding glare of the noonday sun glinted off the chrome of the car.

Ray said, "That was weird."

"Did you think so?" said Maxine.

"Well, she's an odd one."

"Not that odd," said Maxine.

"No, I guess not." Neither made a move to open their door. They stood on opposite sides of the car, looking at one another over the roof.

"You know what I was thinking," said Maxine.

"What?" said Ray.

"It's a crazy idea."

"I think I know what you are going to say."

"Ask her to come with us? I mean, just for a few days. While we drive. Then we could bring her back."

"Yes!" said Ray. "It's a great idea."

"She probably wouldn't come."

"Maybe not. But we could ask."

"It would be fun if she did."

"Yes, I liked her," said Maxine.

"Me too."

"I'll go ask," said Maxine. She took a step away from the car then stopped and turned. She looked at Ray and she was smiling.

"What?" he said.

"Another Ray and Maxine adventure!" she said with a laugh. Ray smiled too as he watched his wife skip through the tall weeds toward the trailer. The whine of the cicadas high in the trees rose to a furious crescendo.

Binary

"So what do you want me to say?"

"Nothing. Forget it."

"No, I'm serious. Nothing I say seems to be right. Tell me what you want. I mean, do you want to be comforted? Do you want advice? Or do you just want to vent?"

Meredith sighed and shook her head. "To tell you the truth, I don't even know anymore. I just don't have anyone else to talk to."

Ian nodded and said nothing. What could he say? How do you tell someone whose world is falling apart not to worry about it? How do you tell them to just suck it in and soldier on? He'd tried everything he could think of to make her feel better, but his words felt like wet sand falling from his mouth, thick and meaningless. It had been this way ever since the fall: since the last real job fell through and nothing else seemed to be on the horizon.

She'd been working a series of temp jobs each more unsatisfying than the last. She had taken a turn at substitute teaching. After that she helped a friend of hers with some writing and editing work, but the friend never paid her as promised. Then there'd been a clerical job at some obscure state agency that had had so many positions cut through early retirements and furloughs and freezes that the few employees left were so demoralized that they took three hour lunch breaks every day, leaving her to answer phones and fool around with Facebook.

"Well, you can always talk to me."

"Really? Do you mean that? Sometimes I get the sense that you are really bored with me and my shit. I mean, who wouldn't be? Fuck, I'm bored with me."

"I'm not bored with you," said Ian.

She looked at him, her head cocked slightly sideways.

"I mean it," he said.

He had a call on hold, six urgent e-mails to respond to, a minor office crisis brewing, and a budget document due to his boss by two (which meant he wouldn't be taking a lunch today—again), when his cell phone rang. He looked at the display, hesitated, then pushed the button.

"Hey, what's up?"

"You are not going to believe this."

"Uh—what?"

"They *fired* me. These assholes fired me."

"Oh, no. I'm sorry, baby."

"Is that all you can say? 'Sorry, baby?' Unngh! I can't believe it. And in the middle of the day. That pissant Fred came over and said,

'Oh, jeez, I hate to tell you this, but we can't afford to keep you any longer.' And then you know what?"

Ian looked at the blinking light on his phone. "What?"

"They wanted me to stay through to cover for their lunch hour. Can you fucking believe that? They fired me then wanted me to cover for lunch." He held the phone away from his ear. "I told Fred to go to hell and I picked up my things and walked out."

"I'm really sorry about that. But, hey, you hated that place anyway, right?"

"Don't you understand? I don't have a JOB. No JOB. What am I supposed to do now?"

"We'll manage. I make enough to cover for both of us for a while. You can relax, retool. This is a blessing in disguise."

Ian's boss appeared in the door, held up his wrist and pointed to his watch, then disappeared.

"I don't expect you to understand. After all, you have a job. How does it feel to be important? I'm nothing. Do you have any idea how humiliating it is to get fired from a temporary job?"

He let that hang in the air for a moment. The phone was silent. Seconds passed. Then more seconds. Ian glanced at the computer where his urgent e-mails still waited.

"Okay, fine," said Meredith at last. "I know you have to get back to work. Sorry to disturb you with my stupid problems."

"Don't say that. I didn't mean—"

"No, it's okay. I have to go home now. I'll figure something out." Before he could say anything else, she had hung up.

On his way home, he expected the worst, but when he opened the door to the apartment, he found her in a good mood. She was at the kitchen table, mug of tea and her work—want ads, note pad, cell phone, laptop, fanned out in front of her.

"Hey!" she said.

"Hey," he said. "Sorry about the job."

She waved her hand at the air. "Ancient history. Like you said, I hated that place anyway. And I decided to take your advice."

"What advice?" he asked, dropping his keys on the table, opening the refrigerator door. There was nothing there now that wasn't there when he left in the morning. Just once he'd love it if she'd do some shopping.

"I decided that I need to take this as a wake-up call. I'm going to completely shift gears. Think about my next step. Find something to do that I enjoy."

He closed the refrigerator door. "There you go. That's what I'm talking about. So what did you come up with?"

"I have a few options here." She leafed back a couple of pages in the notepad and consulted her list. "Here's an opening at a library shelving books."

"Sounds boring."

"I love libraries. In fact, I once considered being a librarian. It would be cool hanging out with all those books, helping people find stuff."

"What else you got?" He reached for the half-empty bottle of wine in the cabinet above the coffee maker, then opened the dishwasher, reached in and pulled out a wine glass.

"Okay. There's a job at a retirement facility."

"Are you serious?"

"Hey, I called them to ask what the person would do."

"And?"

They said they would help in the rec room, they'd wheel the folks in, play games with them, talk to them, that sort of thing."

"The library is looking better," said Ian. He motioned the bottle to her in a want-some? gesture.

"No thanks, I have tea. And you know what else?"

"What?"

"One thing they said you'd do is when it was slow, you'd put together jigsaw puzzles that people donate to be sure they have all the pieces."

Ian leveled a gaze at her.

"What?" said Meredith. "That sounds fun, right? I mean, can you imagine you'd get paid to put together jigsaw puzzles?"

"Jigsaw pieces with one piece missing. Can you imagine how that would feel to get to the end of a jigsaw puzzle and have one piece missing?"

Meredith was silent a moment considering that.

"Anything else?" Ian asked. "After all, you're on a roll."

"Shut up! As a matter of fact, there is. I was saving the best for last."

"I can't wait."

"Okay, but you have to promise not to laugh."

"I can't promise. Okay, I promise. What is it?"

She handed Ian the paper with one listing circled. He read the ad. His eyes rose up to find hers. A grin spread across her face.

"You cannot be fucking serious," said Ian

"I am."

"Santa Claus. You want to be a Santa Claus."

Meredith grinned back at him. "Strangely enough, I do. In fact, ever since I read that ad, I have been thinking that is exactly what I need to do."

"Where's the phone? I have to call the nuthouse and tell them to bring an extra guy with them 'cause you are out of your frickin' tree."

"Ooh. Why? Why *can't* I be Santa Claus?"

"Okay, I'm going to ignore the fact that it is currently September—"

"I was surprised at that too. But I called. They start this early. If they select you, you go on a waiting list. It's complicated. Apparently there are a lot of people who want to be Santa."

"As I was saying: second, you are female, thin and young. Last time I looked Santa was male, fat and old. How convincing could you even be?"

"Hey, where's your willing suspension of disbelief? After all, these are little kids we are talking about. Under all that costume you could be an albino Hottentot and the kids wouldn't know it."

"Yeah, and thanks for reminding me. That's the other thing: the kids. Kids all day long all over you. Greedy little beggars wanting every consumer item known to humanity, their pants full of crap, peeing on your leg. You really want to do that all day long? And in a hot suit with a polyester beard glued on your face?" Ian had completely lost his smile. He drank his Cabernet.

Meredith looked wounded. "I can't believe you have that opinion of children."

"I love children," he said.

"Well it certainly doesn't sound like it. For your information, I happen to love kids and the thought of being part of their cherished lifelong memories of Christmas is something that fills me with joy. I'm not saying it wouldn't be a hard job, but I think I could be a really good Santa and I think I'd like it."

"You'd hate it. Didn't you ever see that movie 'Christmas Story?' Or 'Bad Santa?' Department store Santas are sadistic, jaded sociopaths. You're not near mean enough to be Santa."

"I wish you could hear yourself. You're the jaded, sadistic one."

"Okay, be my guest," said Ian, pouring a second glass of wine. "Knock yourself out. Go out for Santa Claus."

"Oh, I will," said Meredith defiantly.

"Okay, fine," Ian said.

"Fine," said Meredith.

Ian was in his boss's office when the phone rang. He looked at the ID and glanced at his boss, who frowned, but said, "Oh, go ahead. Take it."

Ian nodded, stood up and stepped into the hall.

"I can't talk," he said.

"Well, I got it."

Ian scanned the carpeted corridor past the offices that were all nicer than his to where the receptionist sat at her post in a highly ergonomic chair with a tiny headset in her ear. He imagined that her headset could easily pick up every word of his call, though he knew this wasn't true.

"Got what?" he said, though he had a sinking feeling he knew exactly what.

"Santa."

"Get out! You already got the job?"

"Well, not exactly," said Meredith. "I have to take a class. If that goes well and they think I can do it, they are going to recommend me to be a Santa."

After their bruising argument two nights earlier—since when, the topic had not come up again—Ian chose his words carefully. "Well, congratulations."

"I know you think I'm nuts to do this."

"Uh—"

"I just have to do something so why not this. After all, it's temporary."

"I guess you could say that. The ultimate seasonal employment," said Ian.

"Yes!" said Meredith. "That's what I'm saying."

Ian wasn't sure what she was saying or what any of it mattered. There wasn't much point in dwelling on it. He knew by now that even though Meredith asked his opinion, she was going to do what she wanted to do. One minute later, he was sitting in his boss's office again.

"Everything all right at home, Ian?"

Nosy bastard, Ian thought. "Oh, yeah. Fine. Meredith got a new job."

"Great! Doing what?"

Ian hesitated. He had half a mind to tell him just to see the look on his face. But instead he said, "oh, you know, just—seasonal work. In retail."

The boss looked as if he'd like to ask another question, but Ian stared him down. "Well, good luck to her," he said.

Nothing in the week that Ian had had—indeed nothing in his life so far—could have prepared him for what he found when he pushed open the door to his apartment on a warm night in early November. Even before the door was open, he heard the music, some be-bop jazz in which a honking sax rode wildly on a crest of bass, drums and piano. When he opened the door, the conversation stopped abruptly. He stood in the door and gazed in surprise at two men sitting at his kitchen table and another leaning against the counter. All three were in their forties if not fifties, none fewer than 20 years older than Ian. All three had ruddy reddish complexions and beards. The two at the table wore flannel shirts, jeans and work boots, but the one standing wore and undershirt, suspenders, and the red pants and patent leather boots of a Santa costume. The standing Santa smoked a stub of a cigar and held a highball glass with only some ice in it. The table was full of beer bottles. An ashtray crowded with butts sent up a bluish column of smoke.

"Well, who have we here?" said the standing Santa. "This must be the famous Ian." The other two said nothing, but stared at Ian directly. Standing Santa looked around at his companions. "Up, now, you louts, show a bit more respect. This is Ian. Meredith's husband and the uncontested lord of this castle."

The other men in the room paused in their talk and looked at Ian. A few murmurs of greetings were heard.

"Be it ever so humble," said Ian with a smile.

At that moment, Meredith appeared from the vicinity of the bedroom. Ian thought she looked lighter and more carefree than she had in years.

"Oh honey," she said. "You're home!" She crossed to him and offered him a peck on the cheek. "I hope you don't mind: I invited some of the guys over."

"Not at all," said Ian. "But if we are going to have a party, I need a beer."

"Weh-hell, there's the spirit!" said Standing Santa. "Now, Ian, I brought over a fairly impressive little microbrew that I'm rather fond of called Mutt's Breath IPA. Should be some left there since this lot is too vulgar to care for such refinements. I myself will return to same when I finish this Jameson's chaser."

Ian dug in the fridge and emerged with a dark bottle. "Do all Santas drink this much. I mean, aren't you guys supposed to be in training for climbing up on the roof or something." No one responded.

"Name's Hal," said Standing Santa. Ian shook his hand. "And allow me to introduce my associates, Eddie and Phil." The men looked up at Ian and nodded.

"How ya doin'?" asked Eddie. Neither offered their hand.

"I'm all right," said Ian. "How are you?"

"I'm fine. And thank you for asking," said Eddie. "People never do. Something about the Santa thing. They just think of you as a prop, a cartoon, a cliché. They never think to ask if you're having a good day or ready to slit your throat."

"That's because they don't give a shit," said Phil.

"He has a point," said Eddie.

"I refuse to accept that," said Hal. "I more blame the tendency of people to think that Santa is perennially happy."

"Blame what you want," said Eddie. "But in twelve years doing Santa, it occurs to me that no one has ever asked me how I am doing."

"Shame too," said Hal. "Especially considering that Eddie here is a graduate of the prestigious Charles W. Howard Santa Claus School of Midland, Michigan. You'd think that would command some respect."

Eddie snorted, but he couldn't suppress a grin. Clearly he was proud of his alma mater.

Ian said, "They have schools for Santas?"

Eddie rolled his eyes. "Of course they do. And it's a very rigorous program, too. You'd be surprised. We learned everything from child psychology to how to build a website."

Ian felt strangely disoriented. He took a long swill on his Mutt's Breath. From somewhere far away, he heard his wife's voice. It sounded strangely changed in a way that Ian could not identify. She said: "Eddie is a fireman and Phil is trying to start a record company."

Ian turned to Phil, who swiveled back in his chair and picked up his glass almost as though he were arming himself for an attack.

"What kind of music?" said Ian.

Phil paused before he answered. Then his eyebrows pinched a little inward. "Oh, a little of this and a little of that. Some Celtic, some alt-country. A couple of singer-songwriters and a couple of new-age jazz types. You like music?"

Ian nodded, "Sure. You know, White Stripes, Radiohead, that sort of thing?"

"Um-hmm," said Phil, clearly unimpressed.

"And what do you do, Hal?" asked Ian.

Before Hal could answer, Meredith piped up: "Hal's an astronomer."

"No shit," said Ian.

"I shit you not," said Hal.

"So where did you work?" Ian said.

"Worked," said Hal. "I was at Cal Poly. But I didn't get tenure."

"Sorry," said Ian.

Hal nodded. "Yeah, it's a pisser. They call it publish or perish. Failing the former I was doomed to the latter."

"Did you have a—what do they call it—specialty?" Ian asked.

"In fact, I did. I studied binary stars."

"Wow," said Ian. "That's fascinating."

"Pardon me, but you don't have any idea what binaries are, do you?" Hal asked.

"Actually, no." He found himself a bit bored with this conversation. In fact, all he really wanted was for the three Santas disappear so that he could relax. "I have no idea."

"Oh, boy, here we go again," said Phil.

Hal ignored Phil and said: "Binaries are stars that are locked together in an orbital pattern, usually around a common center of mass."

Meredith helped herself to a beer out of the refrigerator. Ian watched her trying to remember the last time he'd seen her drinking. "Hal says that two-thirds of all the stars in the Milky Way are binary stars. Can you believe that?" Ian looked at his wife like he had never seen her before.

"Right you are, Lady Santa," said Hal. "Binaries are the majority. Single stars like our Sun are the minority. Binaries are cool, though. They just spin around each other for eons, locked into a path of dependence and mutual destruction."

"Mutual destruction." said Ian.

"Well, that's where my research comes in," said Hal. "I'm building computer models to analyze various scenarios for the destruction of binary stars. One model says they will eventually collapse into each other and supernova out, while another model says that they will basically dissolve and spin out into space."

Ian thought about that. "Don't they ever just stay the same?"

At this Eddie, who had been following the conversation without a word spoke up: "Nothin' ever just stays the same. Ain't you never heard of the concept of entropy?"

Everyone looked at Eddie. Hal extended his fist toward Eddie and said, "Hey, Santa Ed, throw me some knuckles, bro." Eddie beamed and raised a fist to meet Hal's.

As November turned into December, Ian watched with something like dismay as Meredith settled into her role as a mall Santa Claus. Or perhaps dismay was not the right or only emotion he felt. More to the point he felt like he was watching something occur to people he didn't know very well. Like he was watching his life from over the backyard fence. She took a job at a mall that was a thirty miles away, but she never complained once about the drive. In fact, to Ian's confusion, the more Meredith settled into her Santa Claus job, the happier she became. She would come home in the evenings, still wearing the red pants, her cheeks rougey red, but stripped down to a t-shirt or blouse on top, and regale him for as long as he'd listen about the children, how cute they were, the things they wanted, her winking distain for the rampant consumerism of the mall and the inevitable tale of a cruel, spoiling, or neglecting parent. Or at other times she would tell of a child whose expectations for Christmas were clearly beyond what the parents could afford. "Eddie taught me this trick," she said. "Glance at the parents and see if they look nervous. And if they do, you do what you can to lower their expectations." Occasionally she would stop and say, "I can't believe how much I love this job." Then she'd say, "And how was your day?" but as Ian launched into some tale of office traumas that even he himself was bored at, he'd notice her eyes glaze over and a slight smile curl the corners of her lips.

For so many years, Ian had watched Meredith as she slogged through life, becoming increasingly unhappy as she descended through one circle of Hell after another, from one dissatisfying job to the next, from one unfinished personal project to another. While Ian had progressed at his company, won the respect of his supervisors and colleagues, and built his self-confidence, he watched as Meredith's career stalled and her sense of self-worth eroded. Often he had found himself longing for the bright cheerful woman he had married seven years before and wondered at just what point she had been replaced by the morose and brooding shade she had become. Long ago they had stopped talking about children or their future and settled into a pattern that carried them from one uneventful day to the next. Often, Ian had found himself wondering if this was all life had to offer and entertaining fantasies of escape.

Suddenly everything had changed. Meredith was once again that light and breezy person of his college days. Suddenly, she was energized, awake, interested. She was reading again. She had resumed her old interest in jogging and was running at least three miles a day. Their sex life had picked up dramatically and he even occasionally—on days that she worked an early shift—found dinner waiting for him when he got home. Ian found himself wondering why this change in Meredith had thrown him so off-balance.

"So, Ian, tell me. What are your goals?"

The question caught him up short. He looked at her. It was after dinner—she had cooked something Italian, creamy and delicious—and they had settled in on the sofa without the television on (the television had been on very rarely lately). It was her night off, perhaps the last until after Christmas. She had warned him that he would see less and less of her as they got closer to the Big Day. Ian had grown quite tired of hearing the wisdom of the Art of Being Santa as channeled direction from Hal and Eddie and Phil through his wife. His wife? It was hard to believe that this changeling was actually still the same person he'd fallen in love with and married those years ago.

"Goals?" he said.

"Yeah. Goals. What are yours?"

He hadn't thought of his life in terms of goals for a long time. "I'd have to think about that."

"*Think* about it? You mean you don't *know* what your goals are?"

"Well, I used to think about writing a novel or walking the Pacific Crest Trail, things like that. . ."

"All-right! That's great! That's what I'm talking about. It's time for you to get back to those things."

"So since when did you get to be so self-directed?"

Meredith looked wounded. "So, what, you liked me better when I didn't have goals of my own?"

Ian flinched. "Goals? Like what? Being Santa at the mall? That's a goal? You've got to be kidding me. What happened to your ideas about being a college teacher? What about the art history book you wanted to write when I first met you? Now those are goals—" he broke off when he saw the look in her eyes. "What?"

"That's the most horrible thing anyone has ever said to me," she said.

Immediately, he moved toward her, but she jumped to her feet. "Don't touch me," she said. Before he could respond, she had fled the room.

Several days later, Ian arrived home with makings for a special dinner. He knew she would be late home from the mall that night. Ever since their fight about their goals, relations had been chilly. Not that they didn't talk, Meredith told him not to worry about it, she had overreacted, but he knew her well enough to know that wasn't right. It still bothered her and he felt terrible about it. He never meant to make her feel bad. A part of him was overjoyed at the change in her of late. And he was intent on drowning the other part of himself in chicken and chorizo in a brandy sauce and thereby winning back himself and the heart of the woman he loved.

Except when he opened the door to the apartment, something immediately felt wrong. Something was gone and it took him ten minutes and a tour through their bedroom to find out. There he noticed that some—but not all—of her clothes hangers were empty. He looked immediately in the bathroom to see that her toothbrush was missing. Only when he went back to the kitchen did he see the note that he had missed before. He stood reading it, then re-reading it for ten minutes.

Then he left for the mall.

The line to see Santa went from the Santa house outside Nordstrom's all the way to Victoria's Secrets. There had to be 100 kids in line at least. Ian went to the front of the line to be sure that Meredith was on duty. At first he couldn't tell if it was really her and realized that he had never seen her in her suit before. But he could tell from her familiar movements that it was Meredith and he had to admit that she seemed to be a very convincing Santa. The little boy on her lap seemed to think so. For a moment, Ian had a strong desire to barge over and shove the kid aside and pull Meredith out of the mall. After all, shouldn't he put an end to this Santa delusion once and for all? Hadn't it done immeasurable damage to their marriage and filled Meredith with false hopes? But Ian noticed how engaged Meredith seemed to be with the little boy on her knee and changed his mind.

He went to the end of the line.

The kids in line stared up at him. He never looked at them, but fixed his eyes straight ahead, aware as well of the glances from the parents waiting in the sidelines. He hoped that no one called for the mall security. He occupied himself with watching the crowd that swirled around him. He watched as teenagers wandered by, the girls in short skirts and tattoos, the boys in baggy jeans and untied tennis shoes.

An hour later he was near the front of the line. The girl in front of him—eight maybe nine in jeans with pink hearts stitched on the back pockets, Hello Kitty t-shirt, bangs and thick glasses—kept looking around at him. Finally, she turned around and said, "What are you doing here?"

Ian thought at first he could ignore her. He continued to stare straight out ahead over the tops of the other kids' heads to where Meredith did her Santa thing with one child after another. Ian marveled at her newfound patience to be able to conduct a nearly identical interview with hundreds of children and still seem to love the job.

"Ex-cuuuuse me," said the girl again, looking up at him through her coke-bottle lenses.

Ian finally looked down. "What?" he said.

"I said what are you doing here?"

"I'm here to see Santa," said Ian.

"But you're a *grown*-up," said the girl. "Grown-ups don't ask Santa for stuff."

"Oh, really? Who says they don't?"

"Well, *do* they? I never heard of any grown-ups talking to Santa. In fact, I don't think grown-ups believe in Santa at all."

"Not believe in Santa?" said Ian. "What are you talking about? Of course we believe in Santa Claus. What's not to believe?"

The girl looked confused. "Well, I still think it's weird you being in line and all. I mean, look, there aren't any other adults in the line."

Ian glanced back at the line. "Hmm. You're right," he said. "Well, there's nothing I can do about that. I have to talk to this Santa and the only way I can talk to her— *him!* is to wait in this line."

The little girl narrowed her eyes at him. Clearly unsatisfied, she shrugged. Then it was her turn. After her meeting with Santa, she skipped past Ian without a glance in his direction.

Then it was Ian's turn. He could see Meredith's eyes watching him as he stepped forward, but under the white beard and mustache, he could not tell if she was smiling or not. He hesitated—was he going to sit on her lap? Finally, he opted to drop to his knees and sit back on his heels.

"Hello, little boy," she said in her best "Christmas Story" Santa imitation.

"Hi, Santa."

"What do you want for Christmas?"

Ian reached into his pocket and pulled out the note. "I want you to take this note back."

He saw then that tears were running down her cheeks and rolling off the top of her beard. "I don't know, Ian."

"What? You can't or you don't know how."

"We've changed, Ian. I'm not that wounded bird you got used to over the last few years..."

"I never thought of you as that."

"But I was. I was. I drifted too far from myself, from the things that meant something to me. I had to find a way back."

"I know exactly. I feel the same way. I just hated it that you found something real before I did. And the whole Santa thing, it was so..." He felt her pull imperceptibly away from him. From out of nowhere, the thought of the binary stars flashed in his mind. Except now he thought the center of gravity was Meredith who had found her own snug and self-contained rotation while he felt himself being flung wildly out into space.

"Is there someone else?" and he hated the hackneyed line even as he spoke it. She shook her bearded head, but he wished he could see her eyes better. He wondered about Santa Hal and Santa Phil, wondered, in fact, about the entire fraternity of Santas and how he was excluded from its mysteries.

"I have to go," said Meredith. By which he understood that she meant he had to leave and she had to stay. He looked behind him at the line waiting to see Santa. He found the eyes of a boy no more than five looking back at him with a very confused expression. He followed the boy's upstretched arm to where it connected with that of his mother and then up her arm to her face, which scowled at him furiously. He held up a one-more-minute index finger at the woman who continued to scowl.

He turned back to Meredith. "Come back to me. I promise. You can be whatever you want with me. I don't care. We'll start over, get back to whatever it was that we used to have."

"Yeah, no, I mean, I don't know. Look. We'll talk about it. But I have to go. I'm at work."

Ian wanted to reach out to her, to touch her gloved hand or hug her red suit, but he knew that such a display would be completely unacceptable. He stood up, nodded, and as he stepped back, the boy rushed forward as though drawn by gravity, brushing Ian aside as he passed.

The Hard Edge of Things

I thought how strange it was to find myself after all these years back in downtown Temple, Texas, with no money on a Saturday afternoon, facing the hard edge of things and no choice about it. I'd hit the limit of what a body could do without a car. The public library closed half an hour ago, and they didn't allow sleeping anyway. I'd been to the park and watched clean-cut guys in shorts pushing their kids in the swings. I walked up one street and down another looking at the empty stores, whitewashed, boarded up. I remembered them when people still shopped there and air-conditioning was new and smelled funny and my mama would buy me a Coke at Mackey's Drug Store. I cupped my hand against the sun and looked through the plate glass where there used to be a department store. A single high-heeled shoe lay sideways on the carpet. I never felt so low.

I made up my mind that minute to walk out to the highway and get out of town, no matter how long it took or how hot it was. But I got stopped after a block by a big freight train passing through, slow as a dream. It had about a hundred cars, so I sat on the high curb to watch it go by. A guy on the other side of the street had the same idea, except he had a flask of peach brandy. He belched and I could smell it and hear it even over the rumble of the train. I read the contents on the sides of the cars: methanol, corn syrup, liquid petroleum gas, gravel. I looked away, up to the big grain silos, and thought how much it looked like Kansas or North Dakota. A black woman came up on the other side of the train, waiting to cross to my side. She wore shorts and a halter top and she had a baby in a stroller. Seeing her flash between the cars as they passed gave an effect like a series of still photos. She looked as hot as me standing there in the sun.

I thought about turning around and heading out South First Street to see the spot where my grandmother's house used to be, that big old house with stained-glass windows and a wide front porch. But just then the last car went by, and I decided I'd head out to the highway like I first planned. There wasn't any point in going to South First anyway, since they'd torn the house down to put in a Diamond Shamrock station and I knew that would only make me feel worse.

So I walked on, down the dusty streets, wondering when they stopped having cabooses on the ends of trains.

Lunch Story

Donna, my boss, leaned against my desk and said, "God, am I the only sane one around here?"

I swiveled in my chair and looked up at her. She didn't look great. The fluorescent lights did not flatter her features. Fluorescent lights don't flatter anyone's features.

"What do you mean, sane?" I said. It wasn't an insightful comment. I didn't mean it to be. I only wanted her to go away so I could make some progress on the pile of work she had given me. My in-basket was literally broken under a leaning tower of papers.

"I just had a cigarette out on the front step with that guy Bosco in Development."

"Bosco?" I said.

"Yeah. I'm sure you've seen him. He's bald and always wears a bow tie?"

"Okay. . ."

"Anyway, it turns out he's a raving Republican racist pig. All he talked about for ten minutes was how *those* people want a handout and *those* people are lazy and *those* people don't take the time to raise their kids."

"Just don't talk to him anymore," I said, eyeing the paper on my desk.

She went on, ignoring me. "I mean, he actually buys breakfast cereal for his kids with candy in it."

"Huh?" I said. None of this was getting any clearer.

"Yeah. He told me this. How his kids eat this stuff that's like Cheerios except that it has candy in the middle. Can you believe that?"

"What do you expect from a guy named Bosco?" I said.

"I mean, here we are trying to change the world and there are people out there using vast creative talents to make a cereal with candy in it."

"They're just hustling a buck same as the next guy," I said.

Donna looked at me coldly and pushed her glasses up on her nose. "Speak for yourself," she said. "It's not a perfect world. When I see something wrong, I have to fix it right now." She put her hands to either side of her head and hunched her shoulders. "Oh, it just makes me crazy," she said.

I picked up a sheet of paper from the top of the stack in my inbasket and tried to look busy.

"Oh, I guess you're actually trying to get something done," said Donna.

"Oh, well. . ." I said. She sighed wearily and drifted out of my office back into hers. I looked at the mountain of paperwork ahead of me and decided to go to lunch. When I passed through Donna's office, she was playing a game on her computer.

I passed the guard's desk in the lobby. It was equipped with an impressive panel of video monitors each showing a half-tone still-life of some remote corner of the building: stairwell, fire door, hallway. Occasionally, a human being, distorted by the fish-eye lens of the camera, would pass elliptically across one of the monitors. The guard, busy trying to work the Times daily crossword in ink, wasn't paying any attention whatsoever to the monitors. He grunted as I passed.

The glass and chrome doors of our building delivered me into the lunchtime crowds on Broadway. The sidewalks were crowded with the motley assortment of humanity typical downtown: men and women in business suits, NYU students in their uniforms of black spandex and leathers, tattered homeless, hitch-stepping hustlers, junkies, deadbeats and drunks.

I headed downtown. I had vague thoughts of going into Tower Records, maybe a bookstore, then catch a sandwich on the way back. At Astor Place, I passed a woman sitting on a heating grate in the sidewalk. She leaned against the building and across her knees lay a sign lettered on a scrap of corrugated cardboard. It said, "my BaBy diEd, Im TRyinG To gEt EnouGH To BuRy Him And Go Back HomE To NoRTH caRoLiNa. PLEASE HELP ME!"

I'd walked by her on that corner for weeks, always with the same sign, watching the crowds walk by ignoring her. I put fifty cents in her blue and white Acropolis cup.

"God bless you, sir," she says to me. I nodded and went on. I wondered where she'd keep it if she really did have a dead baby. I thought of weird possibilities: a locker at the Port Authority, the coat check at the Met. I started laughing to myself.

In the next block a black man with a gray stubble of beard stepped into my path, his hand out. He wore a hound's tooth sports jacket that might actually have once been a fine piece of clothing, taken off a rack in a men's store on the upper East side, now stiff with grime, lining ripped and dangling.

"Spare quatta, spare quatta, spare some cha-a-a-i-i-i-nge!" growled the wino in my face.

I had just donated my last pocket change to the dead baby cause. "Sorry," I mumbled.

"Aii, go to hell, college boy," he said with a wave of his hand, and stumbled away after another victim.

As I approached Fourth Street, the red and orange sign over Tower loomed in front of me. People buzzed in and out of the revolving doors like worker bees around a hive. At the last minute, I decided to pass up the temptation of idle consumerism and turned instead toward the park.

I wandered down Fourth and meandered in a zig-zag north and west through quieter streets past NYU campus buildings and dorms. Halfway down one block, a delivery van was parked with two wheels on the sidewalk, the roll-top back end up and two guys hauling out boxes. As I stepped into the street to walk around it, a deafening shriek filled my ears, echoing down the tight, gray street. A courier on a bike whizzed past me. The whistle in his mouth dropped to the end of its string as the guy yelled at me, "Watch out where you're going, jerk!"

I crossed the street and entered the east side of Washington Square park. The usual crowd was there: roller skaters weaving in and out of the mob, knots of guys around boom boxes, kids in Ocean Pacific sportswear from head-to-toe balancing on the tips of neon green and pink skateboards, fat cops walking around tapping their legs with their nightsticks, old folks on benches throwing popcorn to the leprous pigeons, small children swarming the fenced-in playground.

A skinny guy with polyester pants and sandals, his dreadlocks tucked up under a massive, rainbow-colored macrame cap, stepped in front of me and said quietly, "Weed? Dime bag? Nickel bag?"

I slowed down. I usually had enough sense to tell these guys to beat it.

I hadn't smoked much pot since college, mainly because all my friends had dried up. But I felt loose and a little detached. Without saying a word to the guy, I pulled a ten-dollar bill from my pocket. Like a rasta leprechaun, the guy made the bill disappear, replaced by a tiny zip-lock plastic bag like the Hasidim use to carry rings back and forth across 47th Street or Canal. Inside the bag was enough pot to roll a very skinny joint. When I looked up, the rastaman had vanished.

I stuck the bag in my pocket and went and sat on a park bench. Close by, a crowd had gathered around a guy who was furiously assaulting a guitar and shouting a manic version of "Friend of the Devil."

A dark, attractive woman with short hair and high cheek bones sat down on the bench next to me. She was nicely built and wore black jeans, black T-shirt, black boots and black leather jacket with plenty of zippers and studs. She wore lace gloves with the fingers cut out. Her fingernails were painted black. She took out a cigarette and said to me, "Got a light?"

I fished out my Bic handed it to her. She lit her cigarette, releasing a big cloud of blue and gray smoke. I lit one too and said, "You like it?"

"Like what?" she said.

"The music," I said.

"No," she said. "It sucks."

I nodded. She was right. They guy continued to bang away on his guitar like he wanted to rip out the strings.

"You want to smoke a joint?" I said.

She looked sharply at me and said, "Are you a cop?"

I laughed. "No," I said.

"Well, then. Okay."

"Hold on," I said and went over to where my Jamaican friend was standing with a group of his compatriots grooving to some dub masterpiece rattling out of a boom box the size of a Fotomat. I asked him for a rolling paper. He gave it to me without so much as a glance. I went back to the bench, took out the tiny bag and rolled a joint on my thigh. I lit it from my cigarette and passed it to the woman who took it between the tips of her black fingernails.

"You work around here?" she said.

"Yep."

"What do you do?" she said.

"As little as possible," I said.

She didn't grin. I didn't grin either. She passed the joint back to me and said, "Well, what is it you're supposed to do?"

"I'm not quite sure," I said. I still didn't smile. This was a serious conversation.

"Quite a talker aren't you?"

"Actually, I am," I said. We passed the joint back and forth a few more times until it was gone. I was suddenly high. The guitar player kept pounding away. The park and all its surreal cast of characters seemed to grow small and recede.

"Do you want to walk?" she said.

I nodded and we stood and started off toward Fifth. I couldn't tell which of us was following the other. I wondered how much of my lunch hour was left and whether I could go back at all.

"What's your name?" I said.

"Heidi," she said.

I laughed out loud. I was sure she was putting me on, this dungeon angel in nightcrawler black. But she still hadn't cracked a smile.

"Really?" I said.

"Really," said Heidi.

"I'm sorry I laughed."

"That's okay," she said. "Everyone does."

We walked past the arch and up Waverly toward the West Village. We wandered down side streets past serene brownstones, unchanged for a hundred years, window boxes full of geraniums. I felt very odd and only part of it was because of the pot. I glanced at Heidi walking beside me and wondered if any of this meant anything.

The corner at Sixth Avenue was swarming with activity. Passengers were rushing in and out of the subway and the lunch crowd came and went from the diner up the block.

We turned the corner toward the basketball court.

"These guys are serious," I said. Heidi peered soberly through the chain link fence where ten huge men were playing a noisy, full-court game. Spectators leaned and hung on the fence and kids that should have been in school watched from their bike seats.

"Oh, Jesus, one of those deals," said Heidi. I looked around to see that a crowd had started to gather around a three-card monte game on a flimsy folding table.

The card man laid three bent and worn playing cards face up, flipped them over, mixed them up and put a twenty-dollar bill on the table. "Four of diamonds," he said. "Four of diamonds."

Some guy in the crowd laid a twenty beside the first and turned over the four of diamonds. "All right!" he said, taking both of the twenties. The hustler rearranged the cards and staked a ten. "Four of diamonds," he said to the winner.

"I'll bite," he said and dropped a ten next to the first and pointed to a card: four of diamonds. "Well, goddammit," said the operator. "You doing good." The winner picked up the tens and the house shuffled the cards. This time a fifty appeared: Grant's whiskered, alcoholic face looked up fiercely at this spectacle. Two twenties and a ten met the wager and the crowd was quiet for the brief moment it took to turn over the ace of spades.

"Aw, Christ," said the winner, as he backed away, looking at the ten dollar bill he had in his hand. The hustler swept the bills into his hand and rearranged the cards.

I watched carefully. I was sure it was the card in the middle. Without thinking twice, I pulled a twenty from my jacket pocket, tossed it on the table and picked a card: king of spades. I was dazed. I could ill-afford to lose twenty dollars. Along with the ten left in my pocket, that was all the money I had until payday.

I glanced at Heidi, who looked at me with a bored expression. I didn't care what she thought; I had to get my twenty back. The guy rearranged the cards and put out a ten. I matched it and picked up a card: four of diamonds.

"Yes!" I said. I felt my heart pound as I scooped up the bills. I thought I heard Heidi say "stop now" as I concentrated on the movement of the cards.

Without so much as a pause, I matched the house twenty with my two tens. I was so sure of the cards that I had started to reach for the bills before I realized I was staring at the ace of spades. The hustler's hand snaked out and reeled in my last dime. As I backed out of the crowd, another loser stepped into my place.

I looked at Heidi, who stood with her arms crossed. I could see her trying to decide where to place me on a range of possibilities between kind of interesting and dangerously unbalanced.

I figured she was calculating the risk of involvement by estimating the ratio of interest to misery: a woman's standard measure of a man.

"I have to go back," I said.

We had walked half a block when she said, "Is this, like, a normal lunch break for you?"

"Well, no," I said. "I guess not. In fact, it's pretty weird."

"Hmmm," she said. "I'm not sure if I'm glad to hear that or not."

When we got back to the park, she said, "I have to go this way." She waved her hand northward up Fifth.

"Okay," I said. "Can I call you?"

"No. Give me your number. If I decide to, I'll call you."

I took out a scrap of paper and a ball-point pen, scribbled my home and work numbers and handed her the paper. We stood looking at each other. Her hands were folded in front of her.

Then, with an odd, backward glance, she turned, bounded across Fifth, and disappeared into the crowd. At that moment, high above the honking, screaming, grinding sounds of the city, came the peal of a tower clock; a clear, resounding bong that rang out over the chaos of the city and spoke to me through my confusion.

I began walking briskly toward Broadway. The fogginess of the pot was wearing off. I thought about the oddness of the last hour and tried to puzzle meaning from it. I wondered if I would see Heidi again or if that even mattered. Whatever she decided, in a lonely city full of self-made prisoners of paranoia, an attractive, apparently sensible woman had spoken to me out of the blue without fear or condition or motive. So why, then, had I responded by playing the role of an immature, self-destructive lout, or was that the real me after all?

I dashed though the doors of my building, past the guard who barely glanced at me. As I passed my boss, she was still playing Tetris, the blocks falling like geometric snowflakes on her computer screen.

Without looking up, she said, "Where have you been?"

"Oh, just doing lunch," I said.

"Slow service?" she said.

I suddenly remembered that for all that had happened, I hadn't eaten at all. Nor would I for days if I couldn't find some money somewhere. I chuckled cryptically.

Back in my office, I picked up my phone to check my voice mail. The computer voice told me I had a message, so I punched in my password.

"Hi, this is Heidi. I just want to know if you're as weird as you seem. I mean, it's okay one way or the other. I just have to know. I guess, if you want to meet in the park for lunch tomorrow, that'd be all right. We'll see how it goes, okay? Bye."

I hung up the phone and sat in my office under the unforgiving fluorescent glare.

"Hey, Donna," I yelled into the next office without bothering to get up from where I sat, grinning like a madman. "Can you lend me thirty bucks till payday?"

The Marriage of True Minds

Hector sipped his coffee and checked his watch. Then he checked his watch again. Janice was late.

"You ready for a refill, Doll?"

"Sure, Clara," said Hector.

"Where's that gal of yours? What's her name?"

"Janice," said Hector.

"Ja-neece is it?" said the waitress.

"Yeah. But it's spelled like Janice."

"Oh, lordy," said Clara, shaking her head. "You're stuck on that little gal like a fly on shit. I can tell it."

"I guess. Hey, what kinda pies you got today?"

"All's we got is chocolate cream," said Clara, craning to look behind her, still balancing the coffee pot.

"That's my favorite," said Hector.

"Comin' right up, Sugarfoot."

Clara went to get the pie out of the mirror-backed sliding glass display case behind the counter. Hector looked down the counter, surprised to see someone looking back at him: a girl, 20-something and very cute. If he was to be honest, he'd have to say cuter than Janice—by a lot. She stared at him like she knew him. Did she? Hector tried to remember. He was pretty sure she wasn't in any of his classes at MSJC. It was possible he'd seen her at a party or a friend's house, but then again, this girl didn't look like the kind of gal that would normally be at one of his kind of parties, which was usually just a bunch of his friends hanging out drinking the cheapest beer they could find at the Ranch Market and shooting the shit.

Clara set the pie before him and refreshed his coffee. He fixed his eyes on his pie and ate it in three gulps. He checked his watch again, drank his coffee, studied the lime green check Clara had left beside his plate. Only then did he look back at the girl. She was still looking at Hector—looking right at him and down deep into his eyes—and smiling.

Everything was going wrong for Janice today. She was late to class. Not just any class, but the one with the bitch professor who got really mad when they were late, got mad when they brought coffee into the class, got mad when they shared their homework, got mad when the guys wore baseball caps. The same bitch that had thrown Janice out of class when all she had said was, "WhatEVer! I mean, who's paying for this education anyway?" The rest of the class had thought that was hilarious, but not The Bitch.

She hadn't even cracked a smile, just told Janice to collect her stuff and get out.

Janice was even later than usual today because her favorite parking lot, the one across the street from the Humanities building, was full, and she had to park in the outer parking lot. Then she spilled her latte on the seat of her Focus. Her brand-new Focus, pink with cream upholstery and every extra touch she'd ever wanted in a car, down to the dashboard full of stuffed animals and a license plate holder that read: "I HATE BARBIE--THAT BITCH HAS EVERYTHING." (The only element out of place was the American flag sticker on the back window that her father had put on without even asking her, but what could she say? After all, he was making the payments.)

And then, if all that weren't enough, she remembered that she had forgotten her homework. Homework for The Bitch. Oh, she would get reamed for that, most definitely.

But Janice brightened when she remembered that her class was doing evaluations this week. Oh, she had a thing or two to say. She'd already left some zingers about The Bitch on RateMy-Professor.com, but this time she'd let the university know what she thought. La Profesora thought she was so smart, speaking Spanish better than any of the Hispanic students ever did, better than Hector even. How arrogant! But Janice would have the last word.

Halfway across the parking lot, her phone rang. Hector.

"Baby?"

"Oh, Hector. I can't talk now. I'm running to class. Clase de Español. With the Bee-otch."

"Where were you?"

"Where was I?" Janice asked even as she remembered.

"Yeah, you were supposed to meet me for lunch at Cholo's."

"Oh, shit. I completely forgot. I got busy doing my homework for Spanish and lost track of time."

"I missed you."

"I'm sorry, Hector."

"So, what do you want to do this weekend?"

"Something fun," Janice chirped.

"I was thinking--how about we go to Magic Mountain Saturday?"

"Oh, Hector, could we? I *love* Magic Mountain at night! You'd be the best boyfriend in the entire universe."

"No problem, baby. Friday is payday. Hey, call me tonight, okay?"

"I will. Gotta go. Bye."

As she crossed the street, Janice thought about Hector, about her father, about her friend Monique and Monique's hip-hop boyfriend, Meh-Lo. Brief, dark clouds crossed her mind quickly then vanished just as quickly.

Brad Foster weaved his truck through slower traffic on the 215 south. He was only in Perris with 20 minutes to get to the job site in Temecula, he knew he'd be late. The last thing he needed was to be late; these guys would take any excuse not to pay. And with new home starts nearly stopped and a bunch of foreclosures still out on the market, he couldn't afford to get a bad reputation. He mashed the gas pedal and zoomed past a silver Honda Accord and a green and white Mini Cooper.

His cell phone rang: his daughter Janice.

"Daddy, I HATE my Spanish teacher," she said without preamble, "She's a fucking bitch."

"Hey! Watch your language. Why? What did she do this time?" Brad had heard this before. He moved into the left lane to avoid the back-up at McCall Road.

"Oh, the same. She gets her panties all twisted when we're just five minutes late."

Brad checked his watch and wondered how late he'd be. He tried to think of what his wife would have said in a similar situation.

"I've tried to tell you, angel, these college professors think they're hot shit. They ain't."

"Daddy?"

"Hmm?"

"Why don't you like Hector?"

"What? You think I don't like Hector? He's a good kid."

"Oh, come on. You can't stand him. Is it 'cause he's a Mexican? Or 'cause he drives a rice rocket and works at Toys R Us?"

"He works at Toys R Us?"

"Oh, Daddy, please!"

"Hey, I like him fine, Sweetheart. I just think you could do better. I mean, here you are, a student at a good college, working on a promising career in—what is it?"

"Artist representation."

"Yeah, right. And what is Hector doing? He's in community college and working at Toys R Us. He might not be your match, princess." Brad moved into the left lane and pushed his speed up to 80. "Believe me, I know from experience, you have to be sure."

"He's nice, Daddy. He's taking me to Magic Mountain this weekend. I love Magic Mountain at night."

"Listen, sweetheart, I gotta get moving here. I'm late to a site and this guy's looking for an excuse to kick my ass. I'll talk to you tonight."

"Yeah whatever," Janice mumbled.

Brad turned off the phone and tossed it onto the pile of papers that littered the passenger seat beside him. He consoled himself with the thought that if the high-priced talent he'd hired did their job right, he wouldn't have to worry about Hector for much longer.

Hector had only been at the counter at Cholo's for a couple of minutes when the same babe from the day before walked in. If he didn't know better, he'd think she was following him. As she walked by, she smiled at him with a smile that turned up slightly at one corner and showed her perfect teeth. Hector marveled that a smile could have so many parts. She was beautiful with precise, feminine features, high cheekbones, and clear green eyes. She was more than beautiful, she was hip, with a reckless head of spiky hair, multiple earrings and a ring in her nose.

Hector tried not to glance at her body as she approached: her full breasts and bare midriff, tiny gold ring piercing her navel. And he tried not to watch her as she passed by and walked away, straight back, hip-hugging cargo pants, boots.

She turned and caught him staring at her. Her smile widened, and changed, became conspiratorial.

Hector didn't wait for his coffee. He threw two dollars on the counter and left without looking back.

Janice drove to Monrovia to pick up her friend Monique. Monique used to live in San Bernardino until she met her current boyfriend, the rap star, Meh-Lo (real name: Melvin Lawrence) at the Rose Bowl Parade two years ago when she was playing the French Horn in the Chavez High School marching band. Meh-Lo was sharing a float with Faith Hill (go figure), but picked Janice out of the crowd.

"So how's it going with Hector?"

"Oh, okay I guess," said Janice. "He's taking me to Magic Mountain this Saturday."

"Ooohhh! You're so-o-o-o lucky! I love Magic Mountain. I wish Mel would take me there. We never go anywhere."

"But I don't know. Hector's kind of quiet or something. He just goes to work and school and home. We don't ever do nothing."

"Hey, count your blessings. I wish we ever had a quiet night to ourselves. You know who was over last week?"

"No who?" said Janice.

"Snoop!"

"No shit."

"Serious. He lives in Temecula you know."

"Is he nice?"

"Didn't say much. He and Mel had some business." Monique left the rest to Janice's imagination.

"You better be careful all them rappers shootin' at each other. Tupac and B-I-G and all that." Monique laughed. Janice watched the stores of El Monte fly by. Was that a new TGI Fridays?

"You know Mel is building his new place. It's gonna be great. You and Hector can come out when it's finished. Eight bedrooms, an exercise room, sauna, library, music room."

"Where is that again?" asked Janice.

"Calabasas. Mel says he doesn't want to build his dream house in some dive up in the Valley or Compton or whatever."

"Oh."

"So your dad still hates Hector?"

"Yeah, he hates him."

"That must be hard. I should know. I haven't talked to Mom and Dad for a year. They refuse to call me for fear Mel will pick up the phone. I don't know why they worry. He never answers the phone."

"They're still mad about the CD cover?" asked Janice.

"I guess. But it's not like I was really naked."

"You had a rose," said Janice. "That's all."

"But I was covered."

"Your ass was sticking out."

"Not all of it," said Monique.

"Enough," said Janice.

"So, like, you're doing this artist management thing, right?"

"Go ahead, change the subject."

"So you'll be an agent, right?"

"That's the plan," said Janice.

"Well, you should talk to Mel about that. Maybe he'd give you some pointers. He might put you in touch with his manager, Leon Garfinkle. I mean, Leon's a real asshole, but you'd probably learn something."

"I think you have to be an asshole in that business," said Janice. "But thanks, that would be cool."

"Cool," said Monique, pleased that she had thought of it.

Hector watched Professor Ford as he moved among the students, circulating the handouts. He admired the professor's confident air. Hector thought Professor Ford was no doubt the smartest person he'd ever met, even considering his mother, who was very smart and had been a labor organizer until she got married and had kids. Hector had tried for weeks to guess his age before deciding that he was one of those people who was neither old nor young like maybe he would stay 40-something forever. As he passed by, the professor put Hector's handout on his desk.

"Now I don't want you people to freak out. This is poetry. And not only is it poetry, but it's Shakespeare. Please don't moan and don't roll your eyes. People have been reading this poem for four hundred years. People, actually, who are much dumber than you."

"But I don't do poetry," said a girl in the front row.

"You do today, my lady," said Professor Ford. "And guess what—you'll like it. Now, someone tell me what *form* this poem is written in."

The faces before him stared as wide and still as moons.

"Brandy?"

"Umm. . .yeah?"

"Could you kindly read the title of this poem."

"'Sonnet 116,'" she read.

"Now I repeat. What is the form of the poem?"

"A sonnet?" someone ventured.

"Yes!" shouted the professor. "Who said that? Tanya? Okay, Tanya, you get an A for class participation today." Tanya broke into a huge grin and rolled her eyes.

Hector slid into his seat. He wished he had said sonnet. He had thought sonnet, but he had been afraid to answer for fear he would be wrong.

"Who will read the first sentence?"

Hector straightened in his chair. "I will," he said.

"Good, Hector."

"'Let me not to the marriage of true minds admit—'" He stopped, stumped by an unfamiliar word. "'Im-pe-di-ments.'"

"Impediments!" said the professor. "'Let me not to the marriage of true minds admit impediments.'" He looked around the room. "Now will someone tell me what an impediment is?" The blank faces continued to stare.

"Something that's in the way?" said a kid in the back, a kid who always came to class riding a razor scooter.

"Yes. A road block, if you will. And if you read 'admit' as 'allow' rather than 'confess,' as we contemporary readers are prone to do, he is saying what?"

Hector got it and in a rush, before he could think better of it, he blurted out, "He means, don't let nothing keep soul mates apart."

Silence fell across the students. Professor Ford swiveled toward him and said, "Hector, I am impressed. Thank you. You get an A for the day also. Who wants to read the next line?"

Hector at work: stocking the Barbie aisle and answering questions.

"Do you have Little Mermaid action figures?"

"Aisle four."

"Where are the Hot Wheels?"

"Aisle six midway down on the left side."

"Do you have fake vomit?"

"No, but you could try the Spencer's in the mall."

"Did ya hear they opened a Toys R Us in Moreno Valley? Toys Be Us?"

Hector lived thirty hours each week in a pink and blue world of squawking kids, stone-bored parents, booming loud speakers, and a supervisor named Tom who never seemed to be around until closing time. Hector liked his job, though—much to his surprise. Time passed quickly and the jarring, surrealistic environment didn't phase him. He spent most of his time thinking about Janice, either something she had said lately, things he could buy for her, whether her father liked him or not. But now a new face had started popping into his head, a face he tried to push out, forget he'd seen.

Then, almost on cue, as though thinking about her had conjured her, Hector turned down the Harry Potter aisle and there she was, the girl from Cholo's. She looked at him and seemed surprised, but he could tell in a glance that she had come to the store to find him.

"Hi," she said.

"Hey," said Hector.

"I wonder—can you help me out? My niece is crazy about all this Harry Potter stuff, but I can't decide which action figure to get her. Do you think she'd like—?"

"Hermione," said Hector.

"Really? Not Hagrid? He's so—hairy!"

"She's a girl.   The girls love Hermione.   Or either Harry. Everyone likes Harry."

Well, okay. You're the expert. Hey, don't I know you?"

"I don't think so," said Hector.

"I do too," she said. "You go to that coffee shop over on Central. Cholo's?"

"Oh, okay." said Hector. "Yeah, I seen you there."

"My name's Greta," she said, holding out her small and perfectly shaped hand. Hector hesitated, then took it, averting his eyes from hers. Looking down, he noticed the elaborate tattoos that ran up her arm. One in particular—a strange shape that looked like Arabic or some weird language—was positioned just on her wrist above the back of her hand:

Before he knew it, he'd held her hand a second too long and he jerked it back.

"Hector," said Hector.

"Hi, Hector. That's a cool name. I never knew a Hector before." Greta giggled. She tucked the Hermione doll in its oversized paper and plastic package under her arm. "So—did you ever read those Harry Potter books?"

"Nah. I don't read that much. Mostly poetry." For the life of him, Hector didn't know where that last comment had come from.

"Really? Poetry?" Greta's eyes narrowed slightly. "Well, anyway. They're pretty good, those Harry Potter books. If you don't mind the whole fantasy thing, that is, which I don't. Hey, I could lend you one."

"No, well, I mean that's okay."

"No really. It wouldn't be any problem. What time do you get off? I'll see you back here then."

Hector wished he could close his eyes and walk away. Greta was too much in his eyes and ears. Her smile was too big, her breasts too round, her hips too wide, her pants too tight, her language too smart.

"Hey, you know, maybe that isn't such a good idea. I have a girlfriend."

Greta laughed loudly. "Well, excuse me, Mr. Boyfriend. What? You think I *like* you or what? I just thought you should read these books what with working in the Toys R Us and all."

"Well, I get off at eight."

"Okay. Now we're getting somewhere. Then it's settled: I'll see you at eight." Greta danced off toward the checkout counters.

Hector resisted the strong impulse to glance at her ass as she walked away, then he couldn't resist and looked anyway. He finished his shift deep in thought and punched out at seven sharp, just as scheduled.

In the cool light of his laptop screen, Professor Ford sat in the dark of his bedroom, laptop propped on his thighs.

He typed: "'In me thou seest the twilight of such day as by and by black night doth take away.'"

He waited, his breath shallow, for the response. A short beep, then the words appeared:

"Ooh—that's so sexy. Is that Shakespeare?"

The professor typed again, "Yes. From the Sonnets. But it's not sexy. It's about being old. Nothing sexy there, I can tell you."

He waited. He thought as he waited, *I've given her every opportunity to turn back.*

The reply came without hesitation: "I love older men. Especially nice ones that quote Shakespeare. I'm so aroused by that. I wish I could lie in bed with you all night while you read beautiful poetry to me."

The professor waited so long that she typed, "Are you still there?"

"So how old did you say you are?" The professor typed.

"Sixteen," came the response. "But a very old sixteen, if you know what I mean."

The professor closed his eyes. He opened them and moved the arrow of his cursor toward the little x in the box in the upper right corner of his screen. Once click would end this. He paused and thought about how long it had been since he'd been with a woman. He thought about his wife Linda had left with that asshole from Art History. He thought about the accumulated weight of all those nights alone, about lost tenure at UC Riverside and his endless days at the community college, his clueless students and his annoying colleagues.

He typed: "You like Shakespeare? Well, here's another one: 'Let me not to the marriage of true minds admit impediments.'"

"What's an impediment?" said her message.

"Let's meet," he typed and clicked the send button before he could change his mind.

Janice fished the ringing phone out of her purse. Her bare feet were cold on the tile floor.

"Goddammit," she muttered when she saw the display.

"What?"

"Hey, baby, it's me."

"Oh, hi."

"What're you doing?"

"Oh. Nothing much. Studying. What are you doing?"

"Just got home from work. Wanna go out and get something to eat?"

Janice paused. She looked down at her flat belly. She poked her boobs out to make them bigger. "I don't think so. I have a lot of studying to do for tomorrow."

"Okay," said Hector. "But I haven't seen you in several days. I miss you. I don't understand why we can't spend more time together."

"We will, we will. We're still going to Magic Mountain Saturday, aren't we?"

"Yeah, I guess. Okay."

Janice said goodbye quickly and flipped the phone shut. She ran back to bed and leaped under the covers.

"Who was that?" asked the man in the bed, pulling her cold against his warm skin.

"No one," said Janice.

"You lie, girl. That was your man, Hector. He gon' kill us both."

"No he ain't," she said. "Anyway, you're the gansta. You're the Meh-Lo Man. What're you worried about?"

Meh-Lo laughed. "Yeah, baby. Tha's right. I'm the gangsta. The Gangsta of Love. And don't you forget it."

"You told him your name was—what?"

"Greta."

The young man rolled back onto his bean bag chair, laughing. "Greta? Where'd you get that from?"

"What's wrong with Greta? It's a good name. Short for Margaret, which just happens to be my middle name, in case you didn't know."

The young man hooted and rolled around. He rubbed his belly. Greta sipped from her drink and tucked her legs further up under her on the love seat. This was her favorite spot to sit in when she visited Hank, not because it was the most comfortable, but it had a great leopard skin upholstery that she really appreciated.

"I don't know. I liked it better when your name was Sophie. That was more you. You're more of a Sophie."

"Sophie?"

"Definitely Sophie. Go back to Sophie. Forget Greta."

"Greta and her dark ways," said Greta to no one in particular.

"So tell me, Greta, if it isn't too insulting to your professional pride: why can't you do this guy?"

She squirmed on the love seat. She tried to look bored, annoyed. "Not sure. He seems all nervous when he sees me, but usually by now I have them."

"Always. You always have them by now."

"Okay. Always." She waved her arm in front of her face. "I guess I'm losing my womanly charms."

Hank grinned and rubbed his goatee. "Ah, no. I don't think so. Try another theory."

"Maybe he's gay"

"But he has a girlfriend, right?"

"Yeah. Jah-neece."

"Now there's a white trash name if I ever heard it. Doesn't surprise me, having talked to the dad. Strictly middle-brow. Have you ever seen them together?"

"Never."

"Hmm. Gay maybe. Or..."

"Or what?" she said, leaning forward.

"Maybe he's faithful."

Greta laughed noisily. She fell back in her seat and reached for her drink. "Yeah, right. I'm sure that's it."

"No, no, no. I know it's not likely, but then again, there is always a chance."

"I refuse to believe it," said Greta. She stared at Hank. "Well, we'll see about that."

The man grinned. "Ah. A challenge."

"But—" she stopped.

"What?"

"If for some reason—not that I think it will happen, but—if he doesn't tumble, do I still get my fee?"

The man laughed, a bit more forced. "You know the rule, no lay no pay. And this particular guy is very demanding. He doesn't like your new boyfriend at all and he wants him gone asap. But don't worry. You'll get him. If he likes girls, you'll get him. I've never seen a guy yet that doesn't fall. It is an eternal truth of the business. We're just not made that way. We cannot resist."

Brad pulled over to the shoulder of the 60 in Moreno Valley. He dialed the number he'd written on a sticky note.

"Hello?"

"Yeah, is this Mrs. Allen?"

"Ms. Allen, yes. Who is this please?"

"This is Brad Foster. My daughter Janice is in your Spanish class."

"Oh, yes. Janice. Is she okay?"

"Yeah, she's fine. But you're the one with the problem."

"Excuse me?"

"Listen, Miz Allen. I don't know what you're up to, but she thinks you don't like her. She says you terrorize her every day in that class of yours. She says you have it out for her and—"

"Excuse me, Mr. Foster. I have no intention of discussing any student with you. Period. And don't ever call my home again. do you hear me?"

"I have—" Brad began. He heard the line go dead. "Fucking bitch hung up on me!!" he yelled at no one. He hurled the phone against the floor of his truck where the battery popped off the back and the pieces scattered. "Bitch bitch bitch!" he yelled. "No one fucks with me or my little girl. Do you hear me?"

But she didn't hear him and neither did anyone else, rushing past his parked truck on the shoulder of that Inland Empire highway.

It took all night, but Hector carefully copied out the poem about the marriage of true minds. He copied it in his best printing onto special paper he'd bought at Kinko's. He thought as he worked about how Janice's look of surprise when she would open this card. He'd planned to give it to her Saturday night. He even created a special envelope out of the same nice paper from Kinko's. She would be very surprised. And he was sure she'd love this poem just as much as he did. After all, it was about them.

Professor Ford sat on a bench at the Santa Monica Pier. He looked at his watch then scanned the faces of the crowd that swam around him. Parents with their kids (safe to say at this point he'd never be one of those), young lovers roughhousing playfully, the Vietnamese owners of the greasy spoon across the way, smoking in violation of city codes. None of these were her, but then he was early. He had come early to give himself time to reconsider, to turn back, to go home to his house with its comforting shelves of books, computer, soft furniture, student papers he ought to be grading. What was he doing here at all?

But still he sat while the long hand stepped toward the 12 and his heart beat faster and faster and the crowds offered up no one who could be her.

Then, out of nowhere, a man slid onto the bench beside the professor. A thin and fit mid-thirties man with short hair, jeans, leather jacket. He turned at once toward the professor, reaching as he did into his back pocket.

"Are you Wallace Ford?"

The professor stared at him, thinking at first, "The father!" Then, as the man flipped open the wallet in his hand to reveal a silver badge, the professor knew who he was, knew even as his heart sank and his fear flooded up his back and into his head that there had been no girl, that this guy had been the one responding to his notes.

Ford nodded.

"You're under arrest for soliciting sex with a minor."

A uniform cop had assumed a standing position beside the professor.

"I'm sure there's some mistake. I never asked for sex from her. In fact, there was no her. There was only you. So there was no girl even solicited."

"Well, I'm no lawyer, Professor Ford, but I think it's a matter of intention. At any rate, you can chat with the judge about it. We'll provide all the Love Dog's chat messages for background information. Juries usually get a kick out of those."

Ford groaned.

"If it's any consolation, though," said the cop. "I did appreciate the Shakespeare. That was a real classy touch."

"You stood me up, Hector."

Hector looked up from his pie and Shakespeare. Greta scowled down on him, arms folded, she broke into a smile anyway.

"Oh, hi," he said.

"I went to the Toys R Us at eight and you'd left. I talked to your boss. Tom. He said you were scheduled off at seven. You lied to me, asshole."

Hector shrugged.

"What? That's all you can say? What, you don't like me? Am I inadequate or something?"

"Naw, it isn't that. You're really hot. It's just that, well, I have a girlfriend."

"Oh, yeah? Your Janice? Jah-neece? Well, guess what? Your Jah-neece is a skank. That's right. A skankasaurus."

"A what?"

Greta slid into the chair opposite Hector at his table. She reached into her shoulder bag, pulled out two photographs, and dropped them on top of the book lying open on the table in front of Hector.

"Oh, shit," said Hector.

"Can I brang you innithang, Sugarfoot," asked Clara.

"Do you have any Tension Tamer tea?"

"No, Honeybunch, in all tea we got is the reg'ler Lipton stuff 'cept it don't have no strang."

"That'll be fine."

Hector waited for Clara to leave before he said, "Who is he?"

"His name is Meh-Lo. He's a rap singer. He likes your girlfriend. Apparently your girlfriend likes him, too. Now my question is why don't you like me?"

"How did you get these?"

"Let's just say that's sort of my job."

"You're like a private detective or something?"

Greta looked away. "Not exactly."

Hector's brow creased and he breathed hard. "Look, I don't know who you are or what you want with me, but—"

Greta continued to grin at him, her teeth straight and perfect. She sat sideways to the table, legs crossed at the knee, a generous portion of creamy white thigh showing below her skirt. She kicked her leg out in a rhythmic pattern.

Hector looked back down at the pictures of his girlfriend with Meh-Lo, whose name he had heard many times, the one who was her friend Monique's boyfriend, the hip-hop guy. What was she doing with him? He tried to frame some question in his mind. Finally, he stood, closed the book on the photos, left some bills on the table to pay for his food and walked out of Cholo's.

"Hey, Hector," Greta called. "I'm gonna need those pictures back, dude." The other customers in Cholo's turned to look at Hector, then at Greta. She smiled serenely back at them.

"When the fuck are you gonna make this happen, Hank?" Brad demanded into his cell phone. He stood beside his truck at a construction site in Murrieta. This was his biggest job: 4,200 single family units as far as the eye could see in various stages of completion. Some were slabs only, some framed, some nearly done except for the roofing tiles stacked on the sloped tarpaper roofs. Every single one dressed in its own thin skin of beige color coat. Stuccoville, a friend had called it. Brad didn't know of a single other developer who had pulled permits after this. So it was the last job for a while and Brad worried daily that money might run out before these places were finished.

"We're working on it, Mr. Foster. Hector hasn't responded as expected. But don't worry. We're onto a different angle."

"What angle?"

"Well, let me put it this way, Mr. Foster. Do you care so long as the outcome is the same?"

Brad thought a moment and said, "I guess it's okay. The only thing—I don't want anyone to get hurt. Physically, I mean. Is that clear?"

Hank laughed. "No, not physically. That's not the kind of service we offer, Mr. Foster."

The students sat in Professor Ford's English class watching the door. One of them said, "If he doesn't show by ten minutes after class time, we get a walk."

Another said, "I think you have to wait fifteen minutes."

"Fuck that shit," said another and stood up. "I'm jammin.'"

But before he could leave, a small woman not much older than the students walked in, put her disorderly armful of papers on the desk at the front of the room and said, "Hi, sorry I'm late. My name is Norma Chan. I will be teaching this class for the rest of the semester."

"Where's Professor Ford?" asked Hector.

"I'm not really sure," she said, but Hector noticed that she kept her eyes down when she said it.

"So what's your motivation?" Hank asked.

Greta looked at him a moment and said, "You pay me, remember?"

"Yeah, I know. I pay you. But I mean what is your true motivation? This kind of work isn't for everyone. A gal like you could do anything. You don't have to go around breaking up relationships and sleeping with a lot of random guys. I mean, it doesn't seem to bother you. You seem to almost enjoy it."

She rolled her eyes. "Enjoy it?" she asked. "How could I enjoy it? Or I could say, 'how could I not enjoy it?'"

Hank grinned, laced his fingers behind his head and leaned back in his chair. "Go on," he said.

"You're a voyeuristic bastard aren't you?"

"Well. . .yes, I guess I am."

"Okay. Let me try to explain. First of all, the money is good. And I need the money if I am going to be able to afford to go to culinary school—"

"Or Parsons School of Design."

"Or Parsons. I haven't exactly made up my mind about my true path, but that's a different topic. So, the money's good, but you're right. It is more than that. I mean, sometimes it bothers me that I have the power to truly ruin a person's life. Either cost him a marriage or a girlfriend, or whatever. But then I figure two things. First, those people who the guy thinks they love—well, they are usually the true assholes here. Usually they are the ones who hire you. So these guys are better off without them even if they don't realize it. And second, well—"

Hank sipped his martini. "Yes?" he said.

"Second, I—and I hope this doesn't come off sounding too conceited—but, they get to be with me."

Hank laughed loudly. "Oh, ho! That's good. The queen bestoweth her favors?"

"No I mean it. They get to be intimate with me. Sometimes they even get to have sex with me. And I don't mind it because usually I feel sorry for them. But mostly, I have this really big generous feeling because, you know, it's the best they'll ever have. For most of these guys, it's the best sex they will ever have in their whole entire lives. So it's like a consolation prize. Something they get to keep the rest of their lives."

"Oh, you are much more wicked than I ever imagined."

Greta frowned at him. "Wicked? Why would you say something like that? You're the wicked one. I'm not wicked. I'm a fucking angel of mercy. A really nice angel of mercy."

On Saturday afternoon, Hank pulled up a block from Janice's house just about an hour before he had told her he would come to pick her up to go to Magic Mountain. Her Focus sat right beside her father's white pick-up truck in the driveway, but he knew that her room was on the back side of the house and anyway, she would most likely be in the shower, getting ready to go. Hector parked beside a recycling can in front of a neighbor's bungalow on the winding cul-de-sac in view of her house, but not so close as to be seen. He picked up the envelope that lay on the seat next to him. It was an oversized envelope about eight inches by eight inches, with only the handwritten word "Janice" on the outside. He thought about the contents: a card, handmade on nice paper, with the words to a Shakespearean sonnet written in his best hand. Folded inside the card were the two pictures Greta had given him (the question of who had taken them tormented Hector even more than the pictures themselves) that clearly depicted Janice and the rapper known as Meh-Lo in a state of sexual ecstasy.

After a few minutes of waiting, Janice's father came out of the house, got in the pick-up, backed out of the driveway, and sped past Hector without noticing him. Sheesh, what an asshole, thought Hector. Then he refocused. Hector realized that if he were going to leave this note for Janice, now would be his opportunity. He took his keys from the ignition and with envelope in hand made his way toward Janice's house. As he walked, he muttered to himself the words he had memorized, words that he was not even sure he understood, but that moved on his mind like a spell, "'Love is not love which alters when it alteration finds, or bends with the remover to remove: Oh no! it is an ever-fixèd mark, that looks on tempests and is never shaken.'"

Hector left the card under the windshield wiper of Janice's car, turned and started back toward his own car. Only then, did he realize that his eyes were filled with tears.

Hank found an envelope tucked into the door of his apartment. He recognized the handwriting as Greta's. He went inside, dropped his keys on his retro-70s kitchen table and sunk into the Eames chair.

The letter said:

"Dear Hank, I'm quitting.

"Maybe it was the name thing. Maybe it's that my heart hasn't been in this for a long time. I've been thinking about what you told me the other night how I was out of my depth with this and all the questions you've been asking me about why I do this. I can't answer any more questions like that. Once I thought I knew and maybe if I thought about it some more, I would know, but it just all seems like I'm justifying it to myself and you.

"So I'm through with this. I'm going to do something else now. Follow my bliss. Maybe I'll be a chef. Maybe an artist. Maybe a yoga instructor. I might move to Portland, or out to Palm Springs. All I know is that I can't continue to live like this. It's bad kharma. Worse, it's just bad behavior. So be good, pumpkin. You can mail my last check.

"So long, Hank.

"Namaste --Greta."

Hank stared at the letter, read it again, then started laughing.

Brad was halfway out to the highway when he realized he had left his clipboard at the house. He had to have that clipboard. It had everything on it, all the jobs he was responsible for, deadlines, contacts, meetings, everything. He felt the tension rising in his throat. Sometimes he wondered if he could take it much longer. Single parenting a teenage daughter, working long hours, paying off the house and truck, everyone calling every ten minutes wanting him for this or that or the other thing. Half the time it was something they could do themselves. And when he started to think about the whole picture, the totality of it all began to choke up in his throat. Sometimes it got so bad he could hardly talk over the pounding of his heart. He had thought more than once that he ought to go see a doctor. Then he thought better of that plan. What kind of man can't keep his thoughts and feelings in check? He would sort it out, figure it out.

He pulled his truck up in front of his house. Janice's little pink Focus had not moved. That deadbeat Hector hadn't showed up yet. Thank God. As Brad stepped inside, he called out upstairs to Janice, "Hi, Honey. It's just me. I forgot my papers." No answer, then he heard the water running. Still in the shower. Always in the shower.

He located the silver boxed clipboard on his desk in the den, then flew out the door. Only after he was inside his truck and starting to pull away did he notice the envelope under the windshield of Janice's car. He put his truck in park in the middle of the street and left the engine running as he walked back to his daughter's car and pulled the envelope from behind the blades. He recognized the handwriting right away: Hector.

"Damn," he said. He thought momentarily of putting it back, then walked instead to his truck, threw it and the clipboard into his cab and hurried on to his job. He made a mental note to open the envelope later.

Hector sat in his favorite booth at Cholo's. He looked around at the Saturday night crowd: families with young kids, an old man at the counter, two girls giggling, a kid and a girl on a first date. It felt good to be in his favorite joint, just sipping his coffee and not worried about the time. He told himself that he never did like that damned Magic Mountain anyway.

Suddenly Greta slid into the booth opposite him, filling his line of vision with her streaked hair and her lip stud and her big smile.

"Hi, Hector!" she said. "Fancy seeing you here."

"What do you want?"

"Why do I have to want something, Hector? Why can't I just be here for coffee?"

"I wish you would just go away."

Greta looked around the restaurant. After a moment she said, "Okay, Hector. All I ask is that you listen to my story. It isn't long and it isn't boring, but it's important to me to tell you. One cup of coffee. That's all it will take. But there are some things you need to know and I feel like telling someone. I haven't told anyone in a long time. Okay?"

Hector thought it over then smiled in spite of himself.

"Arright, then. One cup of coffee."

The sky changed from blue to pink to a darker shade of blue. Janice watched it all sitting on the hood of her pink Focus. As she sat, she thought about Hector and her thoughts about Hector changed, too. Her anticipation shifted to annoyance, then to anger, then to resignation. She was clearly not going to Magic Mountain tonight. But she didn't have any idea what she would do with her night. Who would she call? Where would she go? Suddenly, for the first time in a long time, she realized she had no plans.

Kids were playing down the block, their voices drifting over the evening air that grew colder as she sat. Somewhere a dog barked and she could hear a siren wailing far away.

She thought of going inside. She thought of calling Hector on her cell phone. She thought of her father who worked all the time and her mother who was long gone (where would she be tonight?). She thought about Meh-Lo and whether all famous people were like him. She thought about her Spanish teacher and Monique and everyone else she knew. She thought about all of them and their individual world they each carried with them and she liked herself for having thought of that. Then she shivered against the cold and realized at once that it was nighttime and she was cold and alone.

Only then, did she get off her car and go inside.

Knave of Hearts

On his thirteenth day in Atlantic City, Krieder's blackjack strategy began to collapse. Whether those endless hours spent leaning on his elbows at the edge of green felt tables had finally come to roost, or whether this lapse was really the onset of some higher plane of consciousness, Krieder couldn't say. Krieder felt his control begin to slip, but he was powerless to stop it. Or rather, he preferred not to stop it. He had played enough blackjack in the last thirteen days to know that if his game were about to go, well then, he'd better just relax and kiss it good-bye. So Krieder's way of kissing it was to get goofy. And that suited him fine—after all, he continued to win—except for one thing. The pit boss had noticed.

The pit boss was not yet fifty and the size and shape of a truck tire. His greasy hair just reached the collar of his herringbone sport jacket and his black boots matched his black polyester pants. He looked to Krieder every part the cartoon of a Jersey gangster. The pit boss moved over to stand beside the dealer, staring down at the cards. Krieder waited in vain to meet the pit boss's glare with some antic silliness. The blackjack tables were located, along with the baccarat tables, on a mezzanine above the gaudy expanse of casino floor. All the other table players had drifted off to the lounge or their hotel rooms, leaving Krieder alone on the mezzanine. The only sound was the soft clicking of the chip that Krieder tapped on the topmost of an Everest of chips before him on the table.

Krieder bet twenty dollars.

"Deal 'em," said the pit boss.

The dealer did as he was told, pulling the cards from a shoe that held six decks of cards. Krieder got two cards face up: a ten and a seven, the dealer his hole card down and one up, an eight. Krieder stared at his own cards and rubbed his chin, mocking a deep frown. The dealer dealt no more to himself so that Krieder knew he had at least his seventeen. Krieder thought, he has any card nine through ace: 6 out of 13 cards: about half the deck.

"What's your pleasure, Stosh?" Some days before, this dealer had taken to calling Krieder "Stosh." This was not Krieder's name, but he never corrected the dealer. It is the habit of blackjack dealers—and part of their training—to keep up a friendly banter with customers. Krieder understood the pretense, but enjoyed it anyway. Mano-a-mano, as Krieder liked to think of it. The pit boss was another matter.

"Ah, well, give me another," said Krieder. The dealer passed another card to Krieder: a two. The dealer flipped his card: a ten. Krieder's nineteen against the dealer's eighteen. Krieder gathered his chips while the dealer reached for the cards, but the pit boss put his thumb down on Krieder's cards.

The pit boss turned his head up toward the dealer. "He had a seventeen with you standing and still he took another hit." The pit boss shook his head.

The dealer arched his eyebrows at Krieder as if to say, "Cool it, man," and passed the cards again. Krieder ignored the warning and slouched against the table, playing another reckless, winning hand.

All of a sudden, the pit boss said to Krieder. "Pick up your chips and get out of here."

Krieder stared at him through a plume of cigarette smoke. "Why's that?"

The pit boss folded his arms and stared at Krieder.

Krieder knew better than to defend his civil rights then and there so he stood and asked the dealer for a tray for his chips. The dealer bent to get the tray, but the pit boss said, "Don't give him a tray." The dealer froze, then looked at the pit boss with a slight turn of the head. "I said, don't give him a tray." The dealer straightened, expressionless.

Krieder stared at the back of the pit boss turning away, then started to scoop chips into his pockets, the expensive ones first— hundreds and twenty-fives, then fives, then, last of all, the ones. Using all his pockets and balancing two precarious piles in his hands, he managed to carry away every chip.

Krieder sat on a bench facing the black Atlantic Ocean. A chill wind blew over the breakers that whooshed and foamed, a pale ghost in the darkness. He zipped his light jacket, but still was cold. From far away he heard a radio but it was too far to pick out the tune. He decided he'd smoke one more cigarette before turning back to his room. He shook a stubby Camel out of the cellophane and felt like the Marlboro man as he lit it cupped in his hands. The match outside reminded Krieder of a barrel fire.

Krieder thought about the pit boss. He tried to distill his anger into something he could focus, but the contempt of the pit boss was so unaccountable and universal that it seemed beyond Krieder's reach. Even so, his mind ran to violent fantasies. Krieder looked at the closed and silent businesses along the boardwalk: tacky tourist shops, 3-for-$10 t-shirt stores, hot dog stands, toffee stands. It surprised Krieder to find Atlantic City so much like his expectation of New Jersey. It's like Mt. Rushmore, thought Krieder, or the Eiffel Tower. You get there and it looks just *exactly* like you knew it would, only smaller.

The only other person on the boardwalk was a woman walking Krieder's way. Krieder looked back out toward the waves.

After a moment, she stepped up to the rail four feet from Krieder. She pretended not to notice Krieder. He knew what she would do next so he was not surprised when she stepped back to sit beside him. She glanced Krieder's way and seemed to smile slightly.

Krieder took out another cigarette and said, "Would you like a smoke?" The woman nodded and took one. Krieder lit his own and passed the matches. The gleam of the little fire lit the woman's face orange and shadow black. She was older than Krieder first thought, but also prettier in a self-effacing way. She reminded Krieder of the kind of women he had known in college towns. Too old by a few years to be a student. Maybe adjunct faculty, or just a hanger-on, an intellectual wannabe lacking an academic affiliation.

In her baggy pants and mannish shirt she looked as out of place as an Amish family would in Atlantic City where most women wore evening clothes and all women were escorted.

"So what are you doing in this place?" She asked.

"Well," said Krieder, "Mostly I've just been playing blackjack."

The woman raised her eyebrows. "Really. Now. . .how do you play that?"

"Can you count to twenty-one?"

"Well, yeah, I guess," the woman grinned.

"Then you can play blackjack."

"So how long have you been here?"

"Thirteen days."

"What? Really? God, how can you *stand* this place for that long?"

"Stand what?"

"This town. It's wretched. I hate it."

"Why's that?" Krieder asked, knitting his brow.

"Oh, all this, this gambling and this—I mean, you have these big shiny casino hotels with all their cocktail waitresses in their skimpy clothes and the sappy music in the bars and all these poor people sitting on stools at all hours of the day and night blowing their life savings one quarter at a time. It's so phony. No, it's worse than that: it's wrong. Then, two blocks away, there are rows of tired old rooming houses with old men sitting on the front porch all day."

Krieder smiled; he knew that smiling was not the right response, but he couldn't think of any other. He wondered if he should tell her he'd been staying in a ratty motel up the same block from those rooming houses. "Actually," he said, "I kind of like it here. I'm starting to feel pretty much at home."

The music from the radio got louder or else the wind had shifted. He could hear what it was—"I Only Have Eyes for You." He hadn't heard that for years. Who sang that song? The Orioles? No—the Flamingos. It made him feel better, a familiar sound that took him back to a time when he was more sure of himself.

The woman blew out a lung full of smoke and said, "Hmmm. How is it you've been here for thirteen days?"

Krieder began to tell her the whole story, starting with how he lived in New York and worked for the City in one of their many data processing units, then quit one day for no particular reason other than that he'd simply tired of working. He told her about not looking for a job for six months and then not finding one for another three.

She interrupted to commiserate about the hardness of New York where she lived for a year attending NYU. She liked New York okay and had several boyfriends until she began an affair with a professor she didn't particularly like and who was married. The business ended when she got pregnant and took a D in his class.

He told her about taking a job at Verizon where he worked for another six months then quit, this time fleeing not just the job, but the suffocating weight of The City. And so he left for Texas where he'd lived before New York.

And she had left, too, back to Boston, though not back to her parent's home in Newton, but as close as an apartment two blocks from Simmons where she finished her degree. She sketched into her brief tale enough boyfriends, cats, cafes, and afternoons at the

Gardner that to Krieder the story began to gather weight and build interest.

"Did you ever go to a game at Finway Park?" he asked.   "I always wanted to go there."

"No. I don't care for sports."

Krieder laughed shortly. "I sorta figured you'd say that."

He told her about stopping in Atlantic City to gamble for the afternoon and how that afternoon stretched into two days, then four, then thirteen.   He told her about playing blackjack nine, twelve, sometimes fifteen hours at a stretch, and stopping then only for food and coffee and maybe a few hours sleep. He told her about how when he closed his eyes he still saw the cards and when he slept he dreamed of the cards.   He told her about the subtle differences between playing Caesar's, Bally's, Trump Plaza, Trump Taj Mahal, and the Tropicana. He told her about the strategy of the game and how Atlantic City rules differed from Nevada rules and how in Krieder's opinion the New Jersey rules favored the house while Nevada rules favored the player.   He told her about his big winnings and losses, though when she asked, he could honestly say he did not know how much he'd won or lost so far. He ended with the story of the pit boss and how he had thrown him out of the casino.

"Was he polite at least?" she asked.

"No. In fact, he was extremely rude. He wouldn't even give me a tray for my chips. There was no reason for that, for him to try to humiliate me like that. You know what I mean? I was going. I wasn't making a fuss. He didn't even give me a reason for kicking me out. Can you believe that?"

"Do they have to?"

"Have to what?"

"Give you a reason," she said.

"In New Jersey they do. In Nevada they don't. But here they're supposed to."

"Maybe he just thought you couldn't carry all the chips and whatever you couldn't carry, you'd lose."

Krieder cocked his head. "You know, I hadn't thought of that. But I'll bet you're right." Krieder felt much better at once. Perhaps the pit boss's action had been motivated by indifferent greed, not a personal and inexplicable malice toward Krieder.

A group of teens—two couples—came down the boardwalk drunk, laughing and talking loudly. Krieder and the woman turned to watch them go by then the woman said, "I had better be going" and stood up.

Krieder stood up, too. "Hey, I'm sorry if I talked your ear off."

"It's okay. I enjoyed hearing about your exploits."

"I guess I haven't talked to anyone but casino employees in almost two weeks."

"Really. It's no problem. I hope you make it to Texas soon."

"Oh," said Krieder. "Thanks. I'm sure I will."

The woman nodded, smiling, and walked off down the boardwalk. Krieder lit another cigarette, watched her walk away then went off himself in the other direction. He thought about the woman as he walked the six blocks back to his motel. He never learned her name or why she was in Atlantic City if she hated it so much. He wished he had said something more to her, something to make her stay a few minutes more. But Krieder had never mastered the art of fast talk and his way with women was too polite for his own good. He'd rather be accused of anything than being threatening to a woman. And for all of these good intentions, he felt he was now paying the price. The woman was gone and there was damn little chance of finding her again.

Krieder thought he'd try anyway. First thing tomorrow morning he'd scout around, maybe she'd turn up. It occurred to Krieder that this woman was the first thing he'd thought about other than blackjack for the last two weeks. This was Krieder's last thought as he pulled off his shoes and pants and fell into bed with the ugly face of the pit boss filling his head as he passed into sleep.

Krieder woke the next morning at six forty-five, the time he always woke when he worked and then, later, when he didn't have to, but couldn't help it. A thin line of sunlight fought through the crack in the dirty drapes. The room was freezing. When he went to bed it had been stifling hot. He lit a cigarette and crossed the room toward the window. He turned off the air conditioner and yanked down a pull cord to open the drapes. Krieder squeezed his eyes shut against the sunlight. When he could open them again, he saw a stoop-shouldered black man crossing the parking lot. He carried a Styrofoam cup of coffee in his hand.

At that moment, Krieder knew he was done with gambling and would leave Atlantic City that day. He had never really *wanted* to come to Atlantic City, but he came anyway, that old gravity pulling him. Then he thought that before he left he'd look for the woman. So he showered, dressed, packed his bags and loaded his car. He came back inside to check under his bed and around the room for forgotten belongings then went to settle his bill. The motel was run by Indians who had decorated the lobby with framed pictures of colorful Hindu gods, some with many arms, some with serene smiles and teardrop eyes. From somewhere he could hear music playing lightly—Bruce Springsteen of all damn things.

The motel owner took Krieder's money, wrote out a receipt and passed it with the change across the counter. He wished Krieder well with a dismissive gesture and vanished through a beaded partition into the living quarter where his family waited.

Krieder lingered a moment, counting his money. After paying the motel bill, he had just over two thousand dollars, about eight hundred more than when he stopped in Atlantic City. He was glad to see he was ahead since he had been afraid to look at his money while he was gambling. At one point, after three days of blackjack, Krieder knew he had won some money, over fifteen hundred dollars, but he had suffered later wins and losses and feared that most of his winnings were gone.

The motel owner stuck his head out of the beads and said, "Is everything all right, Mr. Krieder?"

"Oh, yeah," said Krieder, smiling. "I just realized I won some dough at blackjack."

The owner smiled too. "Very fine, sir. Free money is always a good thing."

"You're right," said Krieder, and he thought, though he did not say it, "But it wasn't free; I earned every damned penny."

The boardwalk bustled with midday activity. Gulls wheeled and floated, their insane laughter crackling dreamily in the air. The smell of food grilled and fried lifted on the moist air. Krieder watched the passersby: boys with pimples, Italian girls with tight skirts and elaborate hair, kids crawling on the rails, their parents transfixed by the crashing ocean. The rising sun had burned off a morning mist and on the horizon mammoth cargo ships crawled north toward New York and Elizabeth. Krieder stood with his fingertips in his pockets, the arms of his sweater around his neck and tied over his shoulder. He smoked a cigarette and then moved on, bouncing slightly on the balls of his feet, wondering vaguely what he might say to the woman if he found her.

In each hotel, Krieder walked quickly through the casino, checked the lobbies, the restaurants, the gift shops, the cafes. At last he came to the last hotel, the oldest, the finest—the one he'd been thrown out of the night before. He'd hoped he wouldn't have to go into this hotel, hoped by some long shot he might find the woman before he got to this one. But he didn't mind going into the hotel. In the frank daylight, his confrontation with the pit boss seemed long ago and far away.

The woman was nowhere, not in any of the public places and finally, since he checked there last, not in the casino. The casino looked just the same at any hour, red and black and echoing with the fake electronic ching of coins and the dinging of the slots. He had turned once through quickly and started out when he stopped abruptly, his attention drawn to the blackjack table ten feet away.

A woman sat at the same table where Krieder sat the night before—not the woman he had been looking for—and behind her smiling like a man selling cars, was a pit boss, though not the one who chased Krieder out of the casino. This one looked about the same age and he had about him the same slick-haired, pinky-ringed unctuousness of the other, but he was smiling and leaning over the woman as she played. Krieder stood smoking, one hand in his pocket, watching the pit boss and the woman at the table. The pit boss leaned down to drape an arm over the woman's chair.

Krieder could see that the woman had been in the casino for hours though he didn't remember her from the night before. The straps of her mauve evening dress slipped down her shoulders. A clear icy drink in a stout glass sat beside her on the ledge. She had few chips, all ones and fives. Krieder knew he should get out of the casino, but instead he stepped closer to the table.

"This game is really easy," said the woman. Reflexively, Krieder played out the hand in his mind. The woman blurted, "well it's a lousy hand: I'll take another." With that she threw a ten dollar bill onto the table. The dealer looked at the bill as though it were a smelly fish. He said, "In blackjack, bets are placed only at the start of a hand. Your bet stands." He flipped a card from the shoe: a seven.

"Bust," said the woman.

The pit boss looked down the slope of the woman's chest. "Right," he said, smirking.

The dealer, who had also gone over twenty-one, moved to gather the chips.

"Hey," said the woman. "It was a draw!"

The pit boss said, "House wins in a draw." He threw his palms up. "There you go—ain't that a bitch!"

The woman looked at him uneasily, then laughed. Her laugh sounded as edgy as a rusty exhaust fan. He patted her shoulder. "Don't worry. You'll do fine. Just remember: try not to go over twenty-one. That's when you lose."

"I know *that*," the woman said, slapping his shoulder. Krieder couldn't tell whether she was drunk or just acting the fool.

The pit boss laughed. "Sure you do. Hey, you want another drink? That one looks a little watered down."

"Sure, I guess. Are they free?"

"You bet," the pit boss purred. "Compliments of the house."

Krieder shook his head. He watched the woman play and lose three more hands of blackjack. She played with extravagant abandon, tossing twenty, fifty, even hundred-dollar bets on the table in a way that made Krieder wonder if she was mental. She mugged such phony pouts each time she lost that Krieder concluded she must be drunk, rich or both. And all the while, the pit boss hovered behind her, replacing her drinks with fresh ones, watching her lose fifty, a hundred, then three hundred dollars to the house. Krieder watched the pit boss's face tense slightly as the dealer turned over his hole card and sometimes not even then, because he knew the game and knew when she had lost already.

Krieder fought down his better instinct to walk out of the casino, get in his little car and drive out of AC forever, into the wholesome countryside, out of the range of the smarm and sleaze of conniving pit bosses, foolhardy gamblers, and false dealers. But Krieder went instead to sit beside the woman at the table. The pit boss, so chummy with the woman, said nothing to Krieder, but the woman giggled, "Hokay! here's another loser!" Krieder chuckled and nodded.

"Misery loves company," he said.

"Ain't that the damn truth," said the woman. "Misery looooves company," then cackled like the wicked witch. Up close, Krieder could see crow's feet radiating from the corners of her eyes.

"Uh, I'm kinda thirsty," said Krieder to the pit boss. "You think I could have one of those free drinks?" The pit boss stared at Krieder without moving. The dealer was a short round man in black and white clothes who moved nothing but his eyes and these darted on a circuit from the pit boss to Krieder, pausing at the woman, then back to the pit boss.

"Hey, what's the matter with you, honey?" said the woman to the pit boss, "get this man a drink. We're gonna play some blackjack."

"What would you like?" the pit boss asked.

"Oh," said Krieder. "What are you drinking?"

"Geen tee," said the woman.

"That sounds good," said Krieder. "Gin and tonic."

The pit boss gestured to a waitress and in a moment a frosty glass trimmed with a wedge of lime appeared at Krieder's elbow.

"Actually," said Krieder, "I think I'll just watch if you don't mind." The dealer scowled at Krieder, but distributed the cards. He moved in a workmanlike manner, like a waiter in a five-star restaurant. When he was done, the dealer had a six up and the woman had two aces. The dealer took another hit, then another, then stopped. His hand was six, four, eight and the hole card. The woman looked at her cards with mock concentration as though planning her strategy, though to Krieder it was plain she had none.

"I think I'll stand," she said. Krieder nearly jumped. "Uh—no," he said. "I got a lucky feeling about your hand. I think you ought to try a split."

"Try a what?" said the woman.

"A split. You count your aces as elevens, bet again on each hand, and take another hit on each hand."

"Oh, really," She said. "And what makes you the big expert?"

"Nothing. Other than the fifteen hundred dollars I won playing this game for the last two weeks." He glanced at the dealer.

"Well la *ti*," said the woman.

"Say, folks," the dealer prompted. "I don't mean to rush you, but..."

The woman paused only briefly before saying. "Oh, hell, I'll do that split thing. I'll put a hundred on each hand." She found two one hundred dollar bills in her tiny sequined pocketbook and laid them on the table.

The dealer replaced her bet with chips and sent over two cards: a ten on one and a nine on the other.

"Ooooh, weee," said the woman.

"Okay, Mister high roller, what do I do now?"

Krieder looked at the dealer's hand, frowned, and said, "stand." The dealer flipped his hand to reveal a six: a bust.

In that moment, when the dealer tended his table with a curt "congratulations," the woman tilted her head back and released a crystal laugh that seemed unusually pure. And just in that moment, when the woman laughed, the dealer fussed with chips and cards, and Krieder's heart began to lift for what he had done for the woman and against the casino, he felt himself yanked from his chair like a stuffed animal. Even as he felt small bones in his neck pop, one small part of his mind admired the wonderful physics that neither jolted the table nor spilt the drinks. As he flew up from his seat, he saw the face of the dealer, mildly surprised, but turning away, and he saw the face of the woman, speechless in surprise.

So he went, half-walking, half-dragged through the casino, and all the way last night's pit boss cooing to him in a voice as calm as bedtime, "You filthy stinking son of a fucking bitch if I ever catch your ass in this casino...I gotta minda slappa silly shit out of you... you're lucky I don't stomp your sorry ass" and other such regards of the day all the way through the casino. Krieder tried to relax and move with the pit boss so as to take the strain off his back and neck. In the lobby, the pit boss let Krieder collapse to the floor in a heap. The pit boss looked up to a group at the registration desks, a Bermuda shorts, eyeglasses-around-the-neck gaggle of retirees, fresh off the bus from Pompton Lakes, ready for the big town, holding their slot credits, their meal coupons sticking out of their shirt pockets. They looked distastefully at Krieder where he writhed on the floor, reaching for his back.

"We caught him cheating the house," The pit boss explained, straightening his clothes. The oldsters clucked their tongues and offered what-is-this-world-coming-to shakes of their frowsy grey heads and went on their way, already whispering about their first adventure of the day.

"Now get the fuck out of here," said the pit boss. "And if I ever see you in here again, I'll kick your ass for good." And at that, he turned on his heel and walked back toward the casino, apparently unconcerned that Krieder might yet return.

Krieder pulled himself to his feet and moved toward the door. A woman's voice called out to him. Krieder turned sharply, thinking for a moment that it might be the woman from the night before, the angel of the boardwalk, his kindred spirit, thinking that perhaps all of this had been worth it after all. But when he looked up, it was just the grinning smeary face of the woman from the blackjack table, running to him, courtesy drink in her hand, pocketbook flailing from her shoulder on a long thin strap.

"Where you going?" she asked.

Krieder shrugged. "I've got to go sometime."

"Are you going back to the City? I could use a lift."

"Texas," said Krieder.

"Texas?" squeaked the woman. "Why would you want to go *there*?"

"Why not?"

"Hmm. Well, could I get a lift part way with you?"

"I don't think so," said Krieder.

"Why not?"

"Because you like it here."

"I do?"

"Yeah. You're a natural."

"But you know what," said the woman. "I'm in big trouble. You could help me out."

"Yeah?" said Krieder, "how's that?"

"It's my husband. I lost five hundred bucks here since last night. If he finds out about that, he's gonna kill me. I mean it. He's real temperamental."

Krieder looked at her. A fresh group of tour bus seniors passed by, ogling her like free food. "Okay, listen," said Krieder. "I'll make a deal with you. I'll give you the five hundred dollars and give you a ride back up to New York."

"You'd do that for me?" Said the woman.

"Yeah, I'll still come out ahead on my winnings and only be about five hours behind schedule on my trip. But I have one condition."

The woman got a sudden narrow-eyed savvy look and pouched out her cheek with her tongue. "Ahhh, yeah, here we go, huh? Time to play The Price Is Right?"

"Aw, nuthin like that," said Krieder. "My price is this: you don't ever gamble again."

"Never?"

"Never."

"But what do you care whether I gamble or not? Anyway, you just said I was a natural."

"I lied. Look, some people are born to gamble, but you're not one of them. This is really a kind of unwholesome place, when you come to think about it."

"But you won't know if I cheat."

"No," said Krieder. "But you will."

"Okay," said the woman. She stood at attention, her spike heels sunk in the carpet, her right hand held up in an Boy-Scout-oath-taking posture. "I solemnly swear never to gamble again. Now let's get the hell outta here."

Krieder laughed and nodded and said, "Okay, let's go."

They stepped out through the broad sliding doors of the hotel into the balmy breezes of the boardwalk where the slow crowds that moved and swayed gently in a salt-water reverie. Krieder felt free and unfettered and on his way home in a real and figurative way. He looked at the knots of people on the boardwalk and imagined Atlantic City in its innocent Monopoly-board heyday of arm-hooked honeymooners and parasoled bathers.

Ten paces out of the hotel, Krieder stopped cold in his steps. The woman took two more steps then stopped too. Facing them, her head held high, her hair blowing behind her, stood the woman from last night, the woman from the boardwalk. Here she stood, like Lady Liberty herself, while he squired this other lesser female at his side, a woman with whom he had nothing in common, no attraction physical or emotional. And that moment, Krieder felt the weight of every other similar situation of his life, every woman he had let slip away, every day wasted, every book put down in the fourth chapter, every unanswered letter. And still for all of it, Krieder could muster neither self-pity nor regret for the lost days, for the chances gone forever.

"Hi," said Krieder.

"Hi," she said, glancing at Krieder's companion. "You're leaving?"

"Yeah? And you too?"

"Yeah."

"I wanted to—" Krieder paused. "I wanted to tell you I enjoyed talking with you last night."

"Yeah," said the woman, smiling. "Me too."

"Okay."

"Okay. Well. . .I guess I'll see you sometime."

"Sure," said Krieder. "See you sometime."

She passed on and Krieder and the woman continued walking in the opposite direction. Neither of them said a word, and for that, at least, Krieder was grateful.

Acknowledgements

There were a number of people who made this book possible. A mighty thank you to my associates Carlton Smith and Deborah Paes De Barros for their insistence that we really could launch a publishing venture. Many thanks to my good friend Mike Ambrose his deep wisdom and guidance in all aspects of publishing. Thanks to Ben Hatheway for his excellent cover design. For Joe Cohoon who knows a hell of a lot more about black jack than I do. Thanks to the publishers of the small press and literary magazines where many of these stories first appeared for believing in and providing a venue for writers like me. And as always thank you to my wife Catharine, my son Peter, and to my father, without whom I would be lost.

Mark Smith

Mark Smith, a native of Austin, Texas, has been writing and publishing fiction, non-fiction and poetry since 1981. His first book of short stories, *Riddle*, won the 1992 Austin Book Award. His stories have appeared in numerous journals, including *Spider*, *The Pittsburgh Quarterly*, *Sulpher River Literary Quarterly*, *Lone Star Literary Quarterly*, *Epiphany*, and *Intertext*. He lives in Riverside, California, with his wife, Catharine Wall.

www.ingramcontent.com/pod-product-compliance
Lightning Source LLC
Chambersburg PA
CBHW031203260626
47169CB00004B/1231